She Kills Monsters: Young Adventurers Edition

by Qui Nguyen

⫿SAMUEL FRENCH⫿

FOR PRODUCTION INQUIRIES

UNITED STATES AND CANADA
info@concordtheatricals.com
1-866-979-0447

UNITED KINGDOM AND EUROPE
licensing@concordtheatricals.co.uk
020-7054-7298

Each title is subject to availability from Concord Theatricals Corp.,
depending upon country of performance. Please be aware that *SHE
KILLS MONSTERS: YOUNG ADVENTURERS EDITION* may not be
licensed by Concord Theatricals Corp. in your territory. Professional
and amateur producers should contact the nearest Concord Theatricals
Corp. office or licensing partner to verify availability.

MUSIC AND THIRD PARTY MATERIALS USE NOTE

IMPORTANT BILLING AND CREDIT REQUIREMENTS

SHE KILLS MONSTERS: YOUNG ADVENTURERS EDITION received its world premiere Off Off Broadway at The Flea Theater in New York City on November 4, 2011, under artistic director Jim Simpson, producing director Carol Ostrow, and managing director Beth Dembrow; with scenic and lighting design by Nick Francone, sound design by Shane Rettig, costume design by Jessica Pabst, puppet design by David Valentine, choreography by Emily Edwards, fight direction by Mike Chin, prop design by Kate Sinclair Foster, and stage management by Michelle Kelleher. The director was Robert Ross Parker. The cast was as follows:

AGNES... Satomi Blair

TILLY.. Allison Buck

CHUCK..Jack Corcoran

MILES ....Bruce A. Lemon

KALIOPE/KELLY................................. Megha Nabe

LILITH/LILLY................................Margaret Odette

VERA, EVIL GABBI, THE BEHOLDER ....Brett Ashley Robinson

NARRATOR, EVIL TINA, FARRAH THE FAERIE .... Nicky Schmidlein

STEVE .... Edgar Edguia

ORCUS/RONNIE ....Raúl Sigmund Julia

CHARACTERS

(6F/4M)

AGNES

TILLY

CHUCK

MILES

KALIOPE/KELLY

LILITH/LILLY

VERA, EVIL GABBI, THE BEHOLDER

NARRATOR, EVIL TINA, FARRAH THE FAERIE

STEVE

ORCUS/RONNIE

*Note: All actors play monsters when needed.

SETTING

Athens, Ohio and the imaginary land of New Landia.

TIME

1995.

NOTE ON STAGING

Because of the many short scenes, it is recommended that all scene transitions should be done "seamlessly" with small light adjustments instead of any full blackouts to help the play move along briskly.

Prologue

NARRATOR. In a time before Facebook, World of Warcraft, and Massive Multiplayer Online RPG's, there once existed simply a game. Forged by the hands of nerds, crafted in the minds of geeks, and so advanced in its advancedness it would take a whole second edition to contain all its mighty geekery.

And here in the land of Ohio during the year of 1995, one of the rarest types of geeks walked the earth.

A Dungeon Master without fear, prejudice, or a penis. This nerd was a girl-nerd, the most uncommon form of nerd in the world and her name was Tilly Evans.

(Lights come up on **TILLY EVANS***, a teenage girl decked out in full leathery D&D fantasy armor with a cool-ass sword in hand. She is surrounded by a horde of Kobalds [goblin-like creatures].)*

(Suddenly they attack!)

*(***TILLY*** quickly slays each of the monsters with grace and efficiency.)*

(She stands poised over their dead bodies as the **NARRATOR** *continues…)*

But this story isn't about her…

This story is about her sister…

(Spotlight on **AGNES EVANS***.)*

(The following sequence is presented elegantly in either shadow-play or with shadow-puppetry.)

Agnes Evans grew up average. She was of average height, average weight, and average build. She had

average parents and grew up in the average town of
Athens, Ohio with her little sister Tilly.

Tilly however was anything but average.

TILLY. What are you doing?

AGNES. Talking on the phone. What are you doing?

TILLY. Trying to re-animate a dead lizard with the power of
electricity.

AGNES. Oh, okay… WHAT!?!

NARRATOR. Though they shared the same parentage, the
two young girls had very little in common. Agnes being
of average disposition was into more typical things such
as boys, music, and popular television programs while
her sister Tilly became fascinated with the dark arts –
magic, dragons, and the vanquishing of pure evil.

> (**AGNES** *goes to put a CD into a stereo.*)

> (*Ace Of Base starts playing.** *)

TILLY. EVIL!

> (**TILLY** *smashes the stereo with her sword and runs
> away.*)

NARRATOR. As Average Agnes grew and grew, she became
more and more engrossed with transcending her
seemingly permanent state of averageness.

> (*The drab* **AGNES** *transforms from "modestly
> charming" to "magnificent cheerleadery." She loses
> her glasses, her hair gets styled, and she gains the
> power of make-up!*)

However frustrated by seeing her sister's unique brand
of uniqueness…

---

*A license to produce *She Kills Monsters Young Adventurers Edition* does
not include a performance license for Ace of Base music. The publisher
and author suggest that the licensee contact ASCAP or BMI to ascertain
the rights holder to acquire permission for performance of this song.
If permission is unattainable, the licensee should create an original
composition in a similar style. For further information, please see music
use note on page 3.

*(*TILLY *is fighting invisible monsters.)*

Average Agnes made one grand wish during her Junior Year of High School.

*(*AGNES *looks up to the Gods...)*

AGNES. I wish I didn't have such a geeky sister!!!

(Her wish echoes...)

NARRATOR. And so the Gods answered her wish...

By smiting down her young sibling in a car crash.

AGNES. What? NO!

(The shadow puppet of little TILLY *on a bicycle gets hit by a car. As it does, the car transforms into a dragon. The dragon picks up* TILLY's *lifeless body in its jaws and flies away.)*

(Fade to black.)

NARRATOR. But fear not, Adventurers, this isn't the story of that particular tragedy.

No, this is the story of how Agnes the Average learned to finally fight and kill monsters.

(Projection: She Kills Monsters.)

Scene One

(Projection: One Year Later...)

(CHUCK, a geekster teen dressed like a Grunge Rocker roadie. He's wearing large headphones, a flannel shirt tied around his waist, and jamming out to Beck's "Loser" as he sweeps the floor of a "RPG gaming store.")

CHUCK. *(Singing to himself.)*
SOY UN PERDEDOR
I'M A LOSER BABY, SO WHY DON'T YOU KILL –

(Cheerleader AGNES enters and pokes his shoulder which startles him!)

WHOA, WHAT IN THE HADES!

AGNES. Sorry, I didn't mean to scare you –

CHUCK. *(Covering.)* I wasn't scared. I'm a black belt...in Jedi...jitsu.

(AGNES is not impressed.)

AGNES. I'm looking for a Chuck Biggs.

CHUCK. You're looking at him! But my homies just call me DM Biggs cause, you know, I'm "big" where it counts.

(He gives her a "You know what I'm talking about" grin.)

As in MY BRAIN!

AGNES. *(Relieved.)* Oh!!!

CHUCK. Not because I'm fat.
Seriously, it really has nothing to do with body mass index, I actually work out...or plan on working out –

AGNES. I get it.

CHUCK. So what can I do for you...sweet thang?

AGNES. One. Don't call me "sweet thang."
Two. Someone told me you might know a thing or two about Dungeons and Dragons.

CHUCK. Depends if we're talking first or second edition…
PSYCH! It doesn't matter which edition cause my D&D
IQ is plus three hella high!

AGNES. You're very odd.

CHUCK. "Odd" as in hot, right?

AGNES. No.

CHUCK. So what do you want to know about the D and the
D?

AGNES. Well, I have this thingy.
I'm not quite sure what it is.

CHUCK. Well, lemme checkity check it out!

> (**AGNES** *reaches into her backpack and pulls out
> an elaborately decorated notebook.*)

AGNES. Be careful with it. It's not mine.

> (**CHUCK** *takes it and carefully begins leafing
> through the pages.*)

You know, you're not exactly what I was expecting.

CHUCK. What? Were you expecting some nerd? Cause I'm
no nerd.
I got a girlfriend.
From New York.

AGNES. How did *you* meet a *girl* from *New York?*

CHUCK. *(Proudly.)* On a little thing I like to call… THE
INTERNET! You've been on the internet, right?

AGNES. Yeah, like once. At school.

CHUCK. It's the bomb, yo!
I got it hooked up at my house. Top of the line. I'm
talking 56 kilobits per second! If you ever want to come
over and check it out…

AGNES. I'm cool.
So about the notebook…

> (**AGNES** *points at the notebook.*)

CHUCK. Well, it's clearly a homespun module.

AGNES. Clearly. Um, what's that?

CHUCK. It's like a map for a D&D game. An adventure. And this one looks like it's written for one to two players at entry level skills and power designations with –

(Something stops him.)

Yo, hold up. Where'd you get this?

AGNES. It's my sister's.

CHUCK. This is your sister's?

AGNES. Yeah, it was in her locker –

CHUCK. Wait, your sister is Tillius the Paladin?

AGNES. Who?

CHUCK. Tilly Evans.

AGNES. You knew her?

CHUCK. Of course I knew her. Every player here in Athens has been on a campaign with the great Tillius.

AGNES. So you can help me figure out what it all means?

CHUCK. Figure it out? Wait. What do you want to do with this exactly?

AGNES. Well, Chuck. It's a game, right? I want to play it.

Scene Two

(**AGNES**, *in her cheerleader uniform, is walking out to her car with her rather blunt and punk-rockish BFF,* **VERA** *[17].*)

(**VERA** *is also a cheerleader, but clearly not happy about it.*)

(**AGNES**'s *boyfriend,* **MILES**, *runs up. He's carrying his football equipment.*)

MILES. Hey guys, did you see my touchdown?

VERA. Of course we did, marshmallow head.
Or do you think we dress this way because we hate pants?

AGNES. You did great, babe.

(**AGNES** *gives* **MILES** *a kiss.* **VERA** *rolls her eyes.*)

MILES. So what are you doing tonight? Wanna hang?

AGNES. I'd love to, but I can't.

MILES. Why?

VERA. She doesn't have to explain herself to you. She's an independent woman. She can do whatever she wants.

MILES. Why are you a cheerleader exactly? I thought cheerleaders were supposed to be cheery.

VERA. And I thought football players were supposed to have balls.

MILES. Hey!

AGNES. Vera, it's okay. He's allowed to ask.

MILES. So why can't you hang?

AGNES. It's...well...none of your business.

MILES. What?

VERA. You heard her.

MILES. Babe.

VERA. Don't call her babe. She has a name.

(**VERA** *clearly isn't going to back down on this.*)

MILES. Agnes.

What's up?

We always go out afterwards. What's the big?

AGNES. I'm busy.

MILES. Doing what?

AGNES. Stuff.

MILES. What stuff?

AGNES. Nothing.

MILES. Nothing? Wait. So is it stuff or is it nothing? Because before it was stuff and now it's –

AGNES. Don't worry about it.

VERA. You sound like an idiot.

MILES. Did I do something wrong?

I did something wrong, didn't I? Look, I'm sorry. I'll get you flowers. What kind do you like? Roses, daisies, lilacs, carnations, marigolds?

AGNES. You really know a lot about flowers –

MILES. What did I do?

AGNES. You didn't do anything. I just can't hang tonight.

MILES. Why?

VERA. Don't look at me. The boy's persistent.

AGNES. It's…it's Tilly's anniversary, okay?

MILES. Oh. I'm sorry. I didn't –

AGNES. I gotta go.

(**AGNES** *leaves.*)

VERA. Told ya, you should have minded your own damn business.

Scene Three

(**AGNES** *cautiously enters the game shop. There's a table in the middle of the room, but everything's dark.*)

(*The room is decorated to enhance the lair-like quality of the game. Funyuns and Mountain Dew are at the ready.*)

AGNES. Hello? Anyone here?

(*Suddenly, smoke and lights as* **CHUCK** *emerges from behind the game table like a rockstar.*)

(*He's sporting a very fancy Dungeon Master's robe. His hood is up to hide his face.*)

(*As he talks, he drops his wannabe b-boy persona and begins speaking all "wizardly."*)

CHUCK. Greetings, Adventurer! I am Chuck Biggs also know as DM Biggs and I will be your Dungeon Master!

AGNES. You'll be my what?

CHUCK. SIT!

AGNES. Okay.

CHUCK. Before you is a game. A game like no other. One written to test your mind, your cunning, and your badassness.

There's also chips and soda for your snacking enjoyment – but lay off the Twizzlers, those are mine!

Are. You. Ready?

AGNES. I guess?

CHUCK. Then imagine if you will this setting.

(*Suddenly, a spotlight falls on* **AGNES** *as everything goes dark around her.*)

You are standing on the sands of a mystical beachside. To one side of you is the endless ocean, on the other is an ominous dark forest.

And from the distance, a hooded stranger approaches.

(A spotlight falls on a hooded figure.)

AGNES. Oh crap. Okay. Am I supposed to do something here? Like fight it?

CHUCK. Not yet.

AGNES. But you said a hooded stranger approaches. If a hooded stranger approached me in real life, I would totally mace him.

CHUCK. You don't have mace here.

AGNES. So what do I do?

CHUCK. Just chill. I'm still giving you your given circumstances.

AGNES. Sorry.

CHUCK. So you're on a beachside with a dark forest to your right and the endless sea to your left...and then –

> *(The hooded figure turns to* **AGNES** *and walks towards her.)*
>
> *(***AGNES*** *awkwardly raises her fists in a fighting position.)*

TILLY. Welcome to New Landia, stranger. I am –

> *(The stranger pulls back her hood and reveals herself to be –.)*

AGNES. Tilly?

TILLY. Tillius actually. The Paladin.

AGNES. You're in this game?

TILLY. Of course I am. I made it up, didn't I?

> *(Overwhelmed by seeing her sister,* **AGNES** *immediately goes to hug her.)*

AGNES. Tilly –

> *(***TILLY*** *stops her though.)*

TILLY. *(Coldly.)* This is a D&D adventure, not therapy.

> *(***AGNES*** *backs off.)*

AGNES. Sorry.

TILLY. So are you sure you want to do this, Cheerleader?

AGNES. I do. But I don't know exactly what I'm doing –

TILLY. Of course you don't. You're a noob.

AGNES. But I do WANT to do this, Tilly. I know this all this meant a lot to you so I just want to –

> (**TILLY** *does not react to this at all.*)

Right. "This isn't therapy."

> (**TILLY** *looks* **AGNES** *up and down to see if she indeed is serious about playing D&D.*)

TILLY. Okay, Cheerleader.

If you really want to play,

then let's play.

But first you're going to have to meet the rest of our party.

AGNES. What party?

TILLY. Every adventurer has a party. This one's ours. Cue the intro music. Go.

> (*Badass "Matrix"-y* style music begins playing.*)

> (*Suddenly, a leather-clad warrior* **LILITH** *appears in a spotlight. Think Underworld's Kate Beckinsale but with more skin showing. Besides being crazy hot, she sports red eyes, fangs, and wields a very large demonic-y battle axe.*)

First up is Lilith Morningstar.

Class: Demon Queen.

AGNES. What in the hell is she wearing?

TILLY. She acts as our squad's muscle. Whenever you're surrounded by an armada of Ogres, she's the one you want holding the steel. She's a perfect combination of both beauty and brawn.

---

*A license to produce *She Kills Monsters Young Adventurers Edition* does not include a performance license for music from *The Matrix*. The publisher and author suggest that the licensee contact ASCAP or BMI to ascertain the rights holder to acquire permission for performance of any songs. If permission is unattainable, the licensee should create an original composition in a similar style. For further information, please see music use note on page 3

LILITH. Violence makes me hot.

> *(Another spotlight falls on a very pale-skinned and white-haired elf. She's tall, lean, and armed with an elaborately decorated wooden staff. She looks like a supermodel.)*

TILLY. Next up is Kaliope Darkwalker.
Class: Dark Elf.

AGNES. Seriously, does no one here like wearing all their clothes?

TILLY. Along with her natural Elvin agility, athleticism, and ass-kicking abilities, she's also a master tracker, lock-picker, and has more than a few magical surprises up her non-existent sleeves. No pointy-eared creature has ever rocked so much lady hotness.

KALIOPE. I'm in the mood for danger.

> *(**KALIOPE** joins **LILITH** and they begin posing all sexy.)*

TILLY. And then there's –

> *(**AGNES** has had enough.)*

AGNES. Pause! CHUCK!

> *(Spotlight falls on **CHUCK**.)*

CHUCK. Yeah, what's up?

> *(**AGNES** points to the girls who are all suddenly frozen like figurines.)*

AGNES. What is this?

CHUCK. This is your party.

AGNES. My party is a leather-clad dominatrix and an Elvin supermodel?

CHUCK. Dude, don't look at me. This is what your sister wrote.

AGNES. "Violence makes me hot?"

CHUCK. Okay, so there's definitely a certain amount of improv involved…

(**CHUCK** *gives* **AGNES** *an embarrassed smile.*)

AGNES. Behave yourself.

(*He shakes off his embarrassment.*)

CHUCK. Okay. Look. Do you want to play the game or not?

AGNES. Sure, whatever.

(**CHUCK** *throws his hood back on and continues speaking in his wizard voice.*)

CHUCK. And then –

TILLY. There's me. I'm the brains of this operation.
Name: Tilly Evans aka Tillius the Paladin, healer of the wounded and the protector of light.
Class: Awesome.

(**TILLY** *steps up beside* **KALIOPE** *and* **LILITH**. *They fall into a movie poster-esque pose together.*)

(**CHUCK**'s *Dungeon Master voice booms over them from the heavens.*)

CHUCK. Welcome to the Quest for the Lost Soul of Athens. Your mission is find and free the Lost Soul before it is devoured by the dark forces of darkness forever.

(*All the girls high-five each other.*)

AGNES. Seriously, you guys are supposed to be a team of badasses?

(*Suddenly, armed monsters [Wraiths] float in and attack the party.*)

(*In a fast and impressive series of moves,* **TILLY** *and company slay them.*)

Okay, nevermind.

(*The* **ELVIN KALIOPE** *sees* **AGNES** *and approaches.*)

KALIOPE. Curious. What form of creature is this?

(*The demonic* **LILITH** *sniffs her.*)

LILITH. Can I eat it?

TILLY. Lilith, you said you were quitting.

LILITH. I said I'd cut down. I've only had two this week.

AGNES. Cut down doing what?

KALIOPE. Eating the flesh of bad guys.

AGNES. Ew.

(**KALIOPE** *pokes at* **AGNES**'s *cheerleader skirt with her staff.*)

KALIOPE. Why are you dressed so strangely?

AGNES. I'm dressed strangely? You do know you look like a Thundercat, right?

KALIOPE. Perhaps it allows for more mobility.

(*Annoyed by her party being so preoccupied with* **AGNES**, **TILLY** *marches over to get their attention.*)

TILLY. Elf!

KALIOPE. Yes, Noble Paladin Tillius.

TILLY. Any word on Orcus's location?

AGNES. What's an Orcus?

LILITH. Is this your special skill? Asking questions? Yes, that will come in handy.

AGNES. What's your special skill? Being a –

(**TILLY** *steps in between.*)

TILLY. OKAY! Guys, stop it.

(*To* **AGNES**.)

Orcus is a demon overlord of the underworld. If there's a lost soul, he'll either have it or at least know where it is. Kaliope is our tracker. If he's near, she'll know his location.

(**KALIOPE** *pulls out a map and places it on the ground for all to see.*)

(*They all crouch down to look at it.*)

KALIOPE. The entrance to the cave of Orcus is here. But once we reach the cave, neither Lilith nor I can accompany you into it. No magical creatures are allowed into his lair unless they risk being entrapped there forever.

(**AGNES** *is examining* **LILITH** *'s costume.*)

AGNES. Seriously, there has to be more to this outfit, right?

LILITH. You look like you would be delicious with a side of baby.

(**LILITH** *snarls at* **AGNES** *which prompts her to run to* **TILLY.**)

AGNES. Okay! So we're going into a cave? Cool. Let's go!

TILLY. Actually, Agnes, before we can go any further. We're going to have to equip you and build you a character. You can't just walk around looking like that.

AGNES. *(Pointing at* **LILITH.***)* I'm not wearing what she's wearing.

TILLY. You're going to at least need a shield.

AGNES. A shield I can do.

TILLY. So what will be your alignment?

AGNES. My what?

LILITH. Are you good, lawful, chaotic, unlawful, evil?

AGNES. I'm a young Democrat.

KALIOPE. And what will be your weapon?

AGNES. I guess a sword. A regular sword.

(*Pointing at* **TILLY** *'s sword.*)

Like yours.

(**TILLY, KALIOPE,** *and* **LILITH** *are offended.*)

TILLY. This is no regular sword.

KALIOPE. You have to earn a weapon like the one Tillius wields.

LILITH. The Eastern Blade of the Dreamwalker.

KALIOPE. Forged from the fiery nightmares of Gods.

LILITH. Blessed by the demons of Bricken.

KALIOPE. And bestowed upon the warrior destined to vanquish the Tiamat from New Landia.

AGNES. So I can't have a sword like that one?

TILLY, LILITH, KALIOPE. NO!

AGNES. Fine, I'll just take a regular sword.

TILLY. And what will be your name?

AGNES. Agnes.

TILLY. No, what will be your character name?

AGNES. Agnes.

TILLY. Stop being an ass-hat, Agnes.

AGNES. No, I just want to use my name. Agnes. It's less confusing that way.

LILITH. Fine, then it is decided, you are Agnes the Ass-hatted.

AGNES. That's not what I said.

KALIOPE. Agnes the Ass-hatted, welcome to our party.

Scene Four

NARRATOR. *(Voiceover.)* And so it was that Agnes the Ass-hatted and Tillius the Paladin ventured forth into the dark dwellings of the truly evil and quite large in stature ORCUS THE OVERLORD OF THE UNDERWORLD, in search for the lost soul of Athens. But what they found deep in that cave was not what they were prepared for in the least...

> *(Inside a dark cave lit with only torches,* **ORCUS**, *an oversized red demon with large black devil horns sits reclined on a throne of skulls and bones. He is busy watching "Friends" on his demonic television set.)*

> *(***TILLY** *and* **AGNES** *quietly sneak in.)*

> *(***TILLY** *looks at* **AGNES** *and gives her a nod. The two girls jump out with weapons drawn.)*

TILLY. It is I, the great Paladin Tillius, healer of the wounded, defender of lights, and I have come here to –

> *(***ORCUS** *puts up a finger to shush her.)*

ORCUS. Shhhhhhh!

> *(***TILLY** *is confused.)*

AGNES. Um, we're here to fight you?

ORCUS. Yeah, that's not gonna happen.

TILLY. But we've come here to battle.

ORCUS. I know what you've come here to do and I'm telling you it's not gonna happen. I'm busy.

AGNES. This is the Overlord of the Underworld?

ORCUS. FORMER Overlord of the Underworld! I quit.

TILLY. You quit? You can't quit.

ORCUS. Whatchoo talking about I can't quit. You know how annoying it is to always get attacked by so-called adventurers all day and night?

> *(A skinny adventurer named* **STEVE** *barges in.)*

STEVE. Orcus! It is I, the great Mage Steve and I've come here to do battle!

ORCUS. See what I'm saying?

STEVE. I've come to claim the Staff of Suh in the name of –

>*(ORCUS reaches over and grabs said Staff and tosses it over to STEVE.)*

ORCUS. Here ya go, little man. It's all yours.

STEVE. Really? That's all I had to do? AWESOME!

>*(STEVE leaves happy.)*

ORCUS. So what would you like? Treasure? Jewels? Some Cheez-Whiz? It's wicked good.

TILLY. I wish to free a soul.

ORCUS. Sure. Which one?

>*(TILLY bravely steps up to ORCUS.)*

TILLY. Mine.

AGNES. What?

TILLY. You heard me, Orcus. I want my soul back.

ORCUS. Coolio. And which soul would that –

>*(ORCUS takes a good look at TILLY.)*

Oh. Crap. This is a bit awkward.

>*(AGNES grabs TILLY by the arm.)*

AGNES. Wait just a minute, you're the lost soul of Athens?

>*(TILLY pushes AGNES away.)*

TILLY. Orcus, can I have it back or not?

ORCUS. You're Tillius the Paladin, correct?

TILLY. Correct.

ORCUS. Yeah, this is a bit embarrassing but I sorta lost your lost soul.

TILLY. What do you mean you lost my lost soul?

ORCUS. Well, I mean I sorta traded it in for this badass TV/ VCR combo from the, um, Tiamat.

TILLY. What?

ORCUS. Yeah, she was really into it and my old TV completely conked out in the middle of a Twin Peaks Marathon…

TILLY. So you just gave my soul to Tiamat?

ORCUS. TRADED your soul to Tiamat.

TILLY. For nothing?

ORCUS. Not for nothing. Have you ever seen Twin Peaks?

TILLY. Oh God.

> (**TILLY** *sits down completely devastated.*)

AGNES. This isn't good, is it?

TILLY. No, not good at all.

ORCUS. *(Cautiously.)* Are you sure you wouldn't take some Cheez-Whiz instead?

> *(Both girls glare at him.)*

No? My bad.

Scene Five

(**VERA** *is working her after-school job at The Gap. She's the dressing room attendant. And she sucks at it.*)

(**AGNES** *walks in and sits down on one of the dressing room chairs.*)

VERA. So where have you been all weekend?

AGNES. Busy.

VERA. With Miles?

AGNES. No, not with Miles.

VERA. Yo, say what? You went out with another guy?

AGNES. Sorta.

VERA. Whoa. What do you mean "sorta"?

AGNES. It's not what you think –

VERA. I knew it!
This whole "girl next door" vibe you're rocking is all an act. Underneath you're just as much of a freak as the slackers in drama class.

AGNES. That's not true.

VERA. So, "Courtney Love", who is this new mystery man?

AGNES. He's a freshman.

VERA. Holy crap, you're fooling around with a fish?

AGNES. I'm not fooling around with anyone. I'm just playing Dungeons and Dragons.

VERA. Oh, okay – WHAT!?!

AGNES. Don't make a big deal out of this.

VERA. I take it back. You're not a freak, you're a geek!

(*A male customer approaches.*)

STEVE. Do you happen to have this in –

VERA. No.

STEVE. But you didn't even hear the size –

VERA. No.

STEVE. I just wanted to –

VERA. Noooooooooooooooo.

> *(The customer walks away confused.)*

AGNES. You're amazing at the costumer service.

VERA. So how does Miles feel about his girlfriend going geek?

AGNES. He doesn't know.

VERA. What? He doesn't know something about you? Surprise surprise.

AGNES. Why don't you like him?

VERA. 'Cause he's a player.

AGNES. He's not a player.

VERA. Please. He's a jock. He plays.

AGNES. He's a muscular dork who doesn't know how to talk to girls. He's not a player.

VERA. That's just his thing. Some guys come at you all slick and smooth, he charms you with being dopey.

AGNES. Do you really think that'd work?

VERA. He's dating you, isn't he?

AGNES. Can we please change the subject?

VERA. Fine. So what's up with this game? Is this some sort of lame senioritis crisis?

AGNES. I know it's stupid, it's just – I want to know why she liked it so much.

VERA. Oh.

AGNES. I know it's just a game, but…

VERA. So how is it?

AGNES. I honestly don't see the appeal.

All we've done so far is walk around and talk to things. I thought there were supposed to be monsters –

> *(Suddenly everything goes dark accompanied with a loud sound cue.)*

Vera?

> *(**VERA** is frozen. She doesn't respond.)*

AGNES. Vera? Hello?

> *(Suddenly three giant insectoid-like bear creatures [Bugbears] enter the space.)*

Oh crap…

> *(The monsters rush at **AGNES** as **VERA** and the façade of The Gap disappears.)*

> *(They're back in the game again.)*

> *(**CHUCK** calmly moseys into the space as **AGNES** is totally freaked out.)*

> *(She runs up to him.)*

AGNES What the hell's happening?

CHUCK. Three Bugbears are after you.

AGNES. Three what?

CHUCK. Three Bugbears.

AGNES. What the heck is a Bugbear?

CHUCK. What do you do?

AGNES. What do I do? I don't even know what a Bugbear is? Are they bugs? Are they bears?

> *(**CHUCK** sits back at his gaming table and rolls the dice.)*

CHUCK. You examine the Bugbears. They are neither bugs nor bears.

> *(**TILLY** emerges from the woods.)*

TILLY. So this game is mundane, huh? All we do is talk and walk? You want more action?

AGNES. I didn't know things were suddenly going to jump out at us.

CHUCK. The first Bugbear strikes!

> *(It hits **AGNES**!)*

AGNES. OW! Whoa! Wait! Don't I get a turn?

TILLY. You wasted your turn examining the Bugbears.

CHUCK. Which they appreciate. Bugbears aren't used to getting such attention. The second Bugbear strikes.

AGNES. Don't roll that dice!

> (**CHUCK** *rolls.*)

> (*One of the Bugbears slashes* **AGNES** *in the stomach.*)

Ow!

> (*She is bleeding and in pain.*)

Oh God…

CHUCK. You've been damaged.

AGNES. Really? I couldn't tell.

CHUCK. What do you do?

AGNES. I fight back!

TILLY. My character does the same.

> (*A Bugbear slashes at* **TILLY**. **TILLY** *however impressively dodges its attack and impales her sword into its neck. It dies.*)

CHUCK. CRITICAL ROLL! Tillius slays one Bugbear.

> (**AGNES** *turns to one of the Bugbears and raises her weapon.*)

You however swing –

> (*She takes a swipe with her sword as* **CHUCK** *rolls. The Bugbear dodges and cuts* **AGNES** *again.*)

AGNES. OW!!!

CHUCK. – and miss.

AGNES. What? Look at these things! How do I miss that?

CHUCK. The bugbear strikes again.

AGNES. No, no, wait!

> (**CHUCK** *rolls. The Bugbear swipes at her as she manages to dodge out of the way.*)

CHUCK. They miss.

AGNES. Okay, let me think.

CHUCK. You take a turn to think.

AGNES. No, I don't –

CHUCK. The other Bugbear strikes.

AGNES. Come on!

(**AGNES** *tries to avoid the attack the best she can, but gets impaled by the Bugbear's weapon.*)

CHUCK. Huge damage! Agnes is down.

(**AGNES** *looks at the weapon stuck in her. She's in an enormous amount of pain.*)

TILLY. Your character is dying, Agnes. What do you want to do?

AGNES. What can I do?

(**AGNES** *slowly begins losing consciousness.*)

TILLY. Start playing this game correctly.

AGNES. What? How?

TILLY. Stop acting like a sarcastic ogre all the time and I'll help you. Can you do that?

AGNES. …

TILLY. Agnes!

AGNES. Yes. Yes, I can do that.

TILLY. You promise?

AGNES. Yes, I promise.

(**AGNES** *collapses to the ground.*)

(**TILLY** *closes her eyes and hovers her hands over* **AGNES**.)

What are you doing?

TILLY. Just shut up.

(*Lights and magic happen. It's bright, divine, and awesome.*)

CHUCK. Tillius uses a revive spell to restore all of Agnes's hit-points.

You get back on your feet.

TILLY. We now stand side-by-side and raise our weapons.

(**AGNES** *raises her sword.*)

CHUCK. And this is what happens next...

> (*Hard-hitting music begins playing. An elaborate and badass fight ensues as the two girls work together to defeat their adversaries.* **AGNES** *fights impressively.*)

AGNES. Wow.

CHUCK. (*Voiceover.*) You've defeated the Bugbears! Agnes levels up! Gains plus one in being less of a dumbass!

AGNES. Wait, is that really a stat?

TILLY. Yep, totally is. You're less dumb! Yay! Now where's the rest of our team?

> (*Demonic* **LILITH** *and the* **ELVEN KALIOPE** *approach, forcing a reluctant* **ORCUS** *the Demon to walk with them.*)

LILITH. You're not serious, love. We're not actually going to bring Orcus along, correct?

KALIOPE. I must agree with Lilith, getting the worst demon in all the underworld to tote along with us does seems less-than-wise.

> (**ORCUS** *raises his hand.*)

ORCUS. I totally agree. I am bad news. Look at me. I'm red. I got horns. I am totes evil.

TILLY. No, you're coming with us.

ORCUS. Man, you're gonna make me miss Quantum Leap.

TILLY. That's inconsequential.

ORCUS. Inconsequential? Have you seen Quantum Leap? The dude time travels...through time...by leaping INTO different bodies. Different BODIES, yo! And putting things right that once went wrong, and hoping each time that his next leap will be the leap home.

AGNES. That actually does sound interesting.

TILLY. You lost my soul, Orcus, so now you're going to have to help me get it back.

KALIOPE. He knows where your soul is?

TILLY. He gave it to Tiamat.

LILITH. What?

> (**AGNES** *raises her hand.*)

AGNES. Question. What's a Tiamat?

> (**TILLY** *signals* **KALIOPE** *to tell her.*)

KALIOPE. This is Tiamat.

> (*Using magic [AKA a video projection],* **KALIOPE**
> *shows* **AGNES** *the dragon of legend.*)

She is a five-headed dragon that has laid waste to generations of adventurers and civilizations since the dawn. Each of her heads embodies the five different elemental powers of the chromatic dragons – earth, fire, water, wind, and lightning. Many adventures have fought her. All have died.

All, except for one…

> (**KALIOPE** *looks at* **TILLY**.)

AGNES. You fought that?

TILLY. Yes.

AGNES. That's –

TILLY. Useless. I didn't pull off killing her. And now she's stolen my soul for revenge.

> (**LILITH** *storms over to* **ORCUS**.)

LILITH. And you just gave it away!?! I should rip out your insides and dine on them right here and now, you overgrown sad excuse for a demonic entity!

> (**ORCUS** *looks* **LILITH** *up and down.*)

ORCUS. Wait just a minute, don't I know you?

> (*This stops* **LILITH** *dead in her tracks.*)

LILITH. Um…what? No, you must be mistaking me for someone else.

ORCUS. No, I know who you are. You and me, we hang in the same evil underworld. And I don't think your daddy's gonna be too happy you're making time with a Paladin and a human.

AGNES. Who's her dad?

KALIOPE. The devil.

AGNES. That explains a lot.

> (**LILITH**'s demeanor suddenly shifts from total badass to shrinking violet.)

LILITH. Look, please don't tell him, okay? He'll kill me!

AGNES. Wow, suddenly someone doesn't seem so tough.

> (**LILITH** "lightly" backhands **AGNES** sending her flying.)

ORCUS. Don't worry. He doesn't have any love for me either. Your secret's safe with me.

TILLY. Orcus, tell us the location of The Tiamat! Now!

ORCUS. Fine.

Go go Orcus Map.

> (A large elaborately detailed map of New Landia appears out of nowhere.)

Behold my comically large map of New Landia. This is the path you will have to take if you want to face the Tiamat. You must first travel down the River of Wetness to the Swamps of Mushy –

AGNES. The names of these locations are terrible.

TILLY. I was going to go back and give them better names later, but – you know – I sorta died before I could get to it.

AGNES. Sorry.

ORCUS. Then you will climb the Mountain of Steepness to the Castle of Evil where you will find the Tiamat.

AGNES. Seems simple enough.

ORCUS. But to be able to face Tiamat, you will have to first fight and defeat all three of her guardians, the Big Bosses of New Landia.

AGNES. That's less simple.

ORCUS. And each one of them are like totally badass so –
most likely – one if not all of you will die before you get
there. So, yeah, you gotta do that...
OR we can chill out in my cave and rock us some
Thursday Night Must-See TV.
Who's feeling me?
No?
Not even "Friends"?
You guys suck.

> *(Knowing how dangerous this quest will be, noble*
> ***TILLY*** *takes in a deep breath and addresses her*
> *party.)*

TILLY. My friends, I cannot ask all of you to come with me.
The journey before us is too perilous and the prize too
personal for me to expect you to risk your lives. I'm
just one warrior and you all have so much ahead of
you. Please if you do not wish to continue, you have my
blessing to stay here and be safe.

> *(Without hesitation,* **LILITH** *takes* **TILLY***'s hand.)*

LILITH. Tillius, you know as always you have my blade.

> *(***KALIOPE*** *follows.)*

KALIOPE. And my staff.

ORCUS. Seriously, I'm totally fine with just chillin' –

TILLY. You don't get a choice.

ORCUS. Man!

KALIOPE. What about you, Agnes the Ass-hatted? What say
you?

> *(***AGNES*** *looks around at this crazy-ass team and*
> *smiles.)*

AGNES. Of course I'm in.

> *(***AGNES*** *joins the party.)*

LILITH. Good! Then let us kicketh some ass.

NARRATOR. *(***VOICEOVER***.)* And so our team of adventurers
set forth into the wild, following the path Orcus traced

out for them. It was indeed treacherous and they did indeed kicketh some ass...

(Cut to...)

(**MUSIC:** like LL Cool J's "Mama Say Know You Out" kicks in!* A high-energy montage of badassery happens here where we see our party kick ass by killing a a crap-load of different monsters in an assortment of different ways from badass to comedic. It is a cavalcade of D&D beasties. They behead mind flayers, slice up liches, smash umber hulks, crush bullettes, basically kill anything that would excite any geek who's ever played a fantasy game. It is gloriously violent and funny.)

(It culminates with a badass slow motion walk [á la Reservoir Dogs] as the team wipes off monster blood and guts from their outfits.)

---

*A license to produce She Kills Monsters Young Adventurers Edition does not include a performance license for "Mama Say Know You Out." The publisher and author suggest that the licensee contact ASCAP or BMI to ascertain the rights holder to acquire permission for performance of this song. If permission is unattainable, the licensee should create an original composition in a similar style. For further information, please see music use note on page 3

Scene Six

(Lights come up on a beautiful fairy, dancing and singing in the woods [Maybe to a song like TLC's Waterfalls*].)

(ORCUS approaches.)

ORCUS. Aw, look at the little forest faerie!
Hello, little faerie, how are you?

(ORCUS goes to pet the FAERIE, but immediately she decks him in the mouth.)

OW!

FARRAH. Look, you overgrown sack of stupid, just cause I'm pretty doesn't mean I won't mess you up! Seriously, did you see a sign on the way in here that said "Petting Zoo"?

ORCUS. No!

FARRAH. Then please do not try to touch me!

(FARRAH pushes him to the ground.)

ORCUS. I don't think I like that Faerie.

FARRAH. Now get out of my magically enchanted forest before I decide to go all Faerie berserker all over your ugly asses.

AGNES. I thought fairies were supposed to be nice.

FARRAH. Nice? Yo, do I sound Canadian to you? Ain't no one here gonna be nice all the damn time. Faeries are happy. HAP-PY. No one said nice. And I'm brimming like mad with some magical happiness. And guess what makes me happiest? Kicking the crap out of any

---

*A license to produce *She Kills Monsters Young Adventurers Edition* does not include a performance license for "Waterfalls." The publisher and author suggest that the licensee contact ASCAP or BMI to ascertain the rights holder to acquire permission for performance of this song. If permission is unattainable, the licensee should create an original composition in a similar style. For further information, please see music use note on page 3

lame-ass adventurers who decide to trespass on my magically enchanted forest!

AGNES. Look, maybe we should just take the long way around to the mountain?

> *(Hearing where they're going suddenly makes* **FARRAH THE FAERIE***'s wings perk up.)*

FARRAH. Whoa! Hold up. Did you just say you're going to the mountain? As in the Mountain of Steepness?

AGNES. As a matter of fact, yes.

FARRAH. Yo, I didn't know all that. You shoulda said something.

AGNES. We should've?

FARRAH. Y'all must be brave, right?

LILITH. We are.

FARRAH. Courageous.

KALIOPE. That would be an apt description.

FARRAH. So you're going to –

KALIOPE. Fight Tiamat.

LILITH. Vanquish the Dragon.

TILLY. And save my soul.

FARRAH. Man, sorry, I didn't realize all that

AGNES. So are we cool?

FARRAH. Yeah, if I'd known all that, I woulda just killed ya right away instead of wasting my breath talking to ya.

AGNES. Um, say what?

FARRAH. I'm one of the great guardians, dummies.

KALIOPE. But she is but wee.

FARRAH. Yeah, and me and my wee butt is gonna kill the crap out of you guys!

AGNES. Seriously, what could she possibly do?

> *(Adventurer* **STEVE** *enters.)*

STEVE. It is I, the great Mage Steve, and I've come to –

> *(The* **FAERIE** *graphically rips out his throat in one quick move. He dies.)*

ORCUS. Yo, to hell with that noise. That girl is straight up cray cray!

> (ORCUS *tries to leave, but* TILLY *grabs him by the horn to stop him.*)

FARRAH. You've reached the end of your adventure. Time to die, dummies!

> (TILLY *pulls out her weapons. Her team follows suit.*)

TILLY. *(With a smile.)* I'll be your Huckleberry.

> (*From the heavens,* CHUCK *announces the fight like a ring announcer.*)

CHUCK. *(Voiceover.)* BOSS FIGHT NUMBER ONE: FARRAH THE FAERIE VERSUS TEAM TILLIUS.

> (*The* FAERIE *charges at the team of adventurers.*)

> (*Though she is indeed small and cute, she's a total badass and begins beating the crap out of the majority of* TILLY*'s party.*)

> (ORCUS *tries to smash her with his club, but she dodges and kicks him in his demon-balls. He curls over.*)

> (LILITH *and* KALIOPE *swing at her with their weapons, but like an elusive bug she maneuvers past them using what looks like a* FAERIE*'s version of Capoeira. When they miss, she counter-strikes each attacker with a kick to the head.*)

> (TILLY *tries to leap on her back, but she gets smacked in the face by one of the* FAERIE*'s wings.*)

> (AGNES *charges at the* FAERIE, *but gets tossed over its shoulder Akido-style.*)

> (*The heroes are in trouble.*)

KALIOPE. Our skills are no match.

(**LILITH** *looks over to* **TILLY** *and grabs her by the shoulders.*)

LILITH. We need magic. Real magic.

(**TILLY** *nods.*)

AGNES. Wait. What magic?

(**TILLY** *begins summoning a magic spell.*)

TILLY. I call on... MAGIC MISSILE!

(**CHUCK** *enters the space and announces –.*)

CHUCK. TILLY CASTS... MAGIC MISSILE!!!

(**CHUCK** *acting as the missile's puppeteer, sends a large fire ball across the stage in slo-motion.*)

FARRAH. Oh crap.

(*When the missile hits* **FARRAH**, *she slow-motion falls off stage.*)

(*Suddenly, back in real time, an explosion of bloody* **FAERIE** *parts explode back onto the playing space.*)

AGNES. Aw gross.

Scene Seven

(It's the next day.)

(**CHUCK** *is chilling on* **AGNES**'s *front step as* **MILES** *walks up.*)

(Seeing this geeky freshman at his girlfriend's house confuses him. **MILES** *cautiously approaches.*)

MILES. Um. Hi?

CHUCK. Hello.

MILES. What are you doing here?

CHUCK. Waiting for Agnes.

What are you doing here?

MILES. I was looking for her as well.

CHUCK. Cool.

(They both awkwardly stand there for a bit.)

What do you got there?

MILES. It's the new Smashing Pumpkins double disk.

CHUCK. Dude, nice! But I'm not gonna lie, I much prefer the consistency of "Siamese Dream" over the gaudiness of "Mellon Collie and the Infinite Sadness."

(**MILES** *can't stand the small-talk any longer.*)

MILES. Okay, man. Who are you? Why are you here?

CHUCK. Oh, sorry, I'm Chuck. I'm Agnes's DM and you are?

MILES. You're her what?

CHUCK. Oh right. Sorry. I'm not supposed to talk about that. I'm her friend. Her secret friend.

MILES. Whoa, you're my girlfriend's "secret friend"?

CHUCK. Yeah, and you are?

MILES. Her boyfriend.

CHUCK. Really? I didn't know she was dating anyone.

MILES. Hold up, she didn't tell you about me?

CHUCK. Well, that's probably my fault. I keep her pretty busy if you know what I mean.

MILES. Keep her busy doing what?

CHUCK. Fighting monsters, my man. Fighting. Monsters.

MILES. I don't even know what you're talking about. But I do know it probably means I'm gonna have to kick your ass! Right here. Right now. Let's go.

CHUCK. Why?

MILES. Because she's my girlfriend!

CHUCK. No, man! It ain't like that.

MILES. Then what is it like?

CHUCK. We just role-play!

MILES. You what!?!

CHUCK. Look, I got no feelings for her, okay? This is just for fun. I'm just here to help her play out this fantasy. There's no long-term commitments!

MILES. Alright, fish, I'm gonna break you in half!

> (**MILES** *grabs* **CHUCK** *and tries to put him in a headlock. However* **CHUCK***'s actually too big and strong so* **MILES** *can't seem to do anything to him.*)

> (*It ends up looking pretty silly.*)

> (**AGNES** *comes out of the front door, holding a pair of black leather gloves.*)

AGNES. Hey Chuck, look at what I found .,

> (*When the two boys see her, they immediately separate.*)

MILES. Hey.

AGNES. Oh, hi.

MILES. I think I should go.

AGNES. Why?

MILES. You're clearly busy.

AGNES. Oh God, you know about this now, don't you?

MILES. Yeah, I'd say so.

AGNES. You don't think I'm a dork now, do you?

MILES. No, that's not what I'm thinking.

AGNES. Do you want to talk about it?

MILES. No. I'll see you around. Bye.

      *(**MILES** runs off. Maybe crying.)*

AGNES. I'll call you later?

CHUCK. Man. That jock really hates D&D.

      (Seeing the gloves.)

Oooh, nice gloves!

      *(**AGNES** shrugs and puts on her gloves. As she does, she's instantly transported to the D&D world.)*

Scene Eight

*(AGNES looks around and starts calling for her
sister.)*

AGNES. Tilly! Tilly, where are you? Check it out, I got myself
some cool –

*(As she looks around, she catches TILLY and
LILITH in what looks like some sort of scuffle. The
two girls are pushing and grappling with each
other. It looks pretty physical.)*

*(Seeing this, AGNES pulls out her blade and starts
approaching.)*

*(But before she reaches them, LILITH grabs TILLY
by the head and starts aggressively…making out
with her.)*

Whoa, what the hell!?!

*(Hearing AGNES, TILLY and LILITH abruptly
separate.)*

TILLY. Oh, hey there, Agnes. Nice gloves.

AGNES. What were you two doing?

TILLY. I was, uh…kissing my girlfriend.

AGNES. Whoa! Wait just a minute! You two are a couple?

LILITH. Does this upset you, lunch meat?

AGNES. It upsets me that you don't know how to put on all
your clothes.

LILITH. I'd advise not talking to me in such a tone.

AGNES. And I'd advise wearing a complete shirt next time
you're MAKING OUT WITH MY SISTER!
Wait just minute, what is happening here?

TILLY. I told you. We're lovers.

AGNES. You're gay?

TILLY. Does that matter?

*(Realizing that this indeed bothers AGNES, LILITH
chuckles.)*

LILITH. Wow, looks like I'm not the only monster here.

AGNES. Get away from me!

> (**AGNES** *walks away from them.* **TILLY** *follows.*)

TILLY. Wow, I never took you for a homophobe.

AGNES. I'm not a homophobe!

TILLY. That's not what it looks like to me.

AGNES. Shut up. I watch the Real World, I listen to Madonna, there's no way I'm anti-gay.

TILLY. Then what's your damage?

AGNES. What's with not giving your girlfriend a full costume?

TILLY. She's a she-devil.

AGNES. She's dirty.

TILLY. I didn't think this would upset you like it does.

AGNES. I thought I knew you, Tilly. At least good enough to know whether you dug boys or girls at this point in your life.

TILLY. You were busy.

AGNES. Not too busy to know this!
I'm your sister. I shouldn't have to learn about you through a role-playing game!

> (**AGNES** *turns away in a huff.*)

> (**TILLY** *cautiously approaches.*)

TILLY. Well, don't worry. You haven't learned anything.

AGNES. What's that supposed to mean?

> (**CHUCK** *appears at his D&D table.*)

CHUCK. Tillius is a guy character.

AGNES. What?

CHUCK. Tillius is a guy.

> (**AGNES** *looks at* **TILLY** *who is now frozen in the moment.*)

AGNES. But she doesn't look like a guy.

CHUCK. That's because you're imagining your sister's character as your actual little sister. But when Tilly played the game, she thought of herself as some dude. Named Tillius. Who was a guy.

AGNES. Why would she do that?

CHUCK. I don't know. Why do gamer dudes always play girl characters like Chun Li?

AGNES. Who's Chun Li?

TILLY. Yo, that's geek blasphemy! You need to go get yourself a Super Nintendo STAT!

AGNES. Wait, so does this mean Tilly's not...um, you know.

(CHUCK *doesn't know how to answer this.*)

CHUCK. Look maybe you should just get back to the game and not worry about that stuff. It's not really part of the adventure. You weren't supposed to get hung up on that particular detail.

AGNES. Uh, okay.

Where were we?

CHUCK. You're back on the road. And you're looking for your party that's mysteriously disappeared.

(CHUCK *rolls the dice...*)

(*The action resumes.*)

TILLY. *(Calling.)* Lilith! Kaliope! Orcus!

Where are they?

(AGNES *looks around and spots them.*)

AGNES. Oh. They're right over there! Taking a nap.

TILLY. Um. Elves and demons don't sleep.

AGNES. They don't? So I guess them being unconscious would be a bad thing, right?

(*Suddenly, a huge pyrotechnic explosion as two evil cheerleaders fly onto the area with an impressive musical number backing them up.*)

(They look like normal cheerleaders, except they have all black eyes, bat wings, and blood all over their mouths.)

TILLY. Oh crap.

AGNES. What?

TILLY. Succubus!

AGNES. Suck you what?

TILLY. Succubus. Demon girls from the demon world who like to do demonic things like sucking.

AGNES. Are they a boss?

TILLY. No. They're just really mean.

AGNES. So do we fight them?

TILLY. No, we run. GO!!!

(They try to run away, but TILLY *gets cornered.)*

EVIL GABBI. Not so fast there, nerd.

*(*TILLY, *though still dressed like her badass self, starts shrinking into her average everyday geek-girl persona.)*

TILLY. Hey guys, what's up?

EVIL TINA. Were you just looking at me?

TILLY. No. Not specifically. I was just looking, you know, in your general direction and then you stepped into my line of…fleeing.

EVIL GABBI. I think she's lying.

EVIL TINA. I hate liars.

TILLY. I'm not lying!

AGNES. Hey, what are you guys doing?

*(*AGNES *marches right up to the two bullies.* EVIL TINA *however grabs* AGNES *by the throat and just holds her there.)*

Ah!

TILLY. Let her go!

EVIL GABBI. I think the reason why she was looking at you, Evil Tina, is because she has the hots for you.

TILLY. That's not true.

EVIL TINA. Are you saying I'm ugly?

TILLY. No.

EVIL TINA. Then do you think I'm pretty?

TILLY. Uh…

EVIL TINA. I don't understand "uh." I don't speak "uh."

> (**EVIL TINA** *begins bearing down on* **AGNES.***)*

AGNES. Owwww!

EVIL TINA. I don't speak "ow" either.

TILLY. No, I do I do! I think you're very pretty, you're so pretty!

EVIL TINA. Of course you think I'm pretty…dyke!

> (**EVIL GABBI,** *pretending to be nice, approaches the very scared and intimidated* **TILLY.***)*

EVIL GABBI. Sorry, Evil Tina is just really sensitive about her looks.

EVIL TINA. Shut up, Evil Gabbi!

EVIL GABBI. She doesn't mean to be mean to you. I like you. I do. Do you want to join our club?

TILLY. What club is that?

EVIL GABBI. The awesome Evil Club!

TILLY. Uh…

EVIL TINA. Again with the "uh's"!

AGNES. Owwww!

TILLY. I would love to join.

EVIL GABBI. Okay! Sit right here and don't turn around.

> (**EVIL TINA** *and* **EVIL GABBI** *start whispering and laughing with each other as* **TILLY** *sits staring in the opposite direction.*)

> (*As she stands there,* **TILLY** *no longer looks like an awesome D&D warrior. She now looks like a normal geeky fifteen-year-old getting picked on.*)

> (*She tries to sneak a peek.*)

EVIL GABBI I said not to turn around, DYKE!

TILLY. I'm sorry, I'm sorry.

> (**EVIL TINA** *and* **EVIL GABBI** *come up with a plan. They giggle and look at* **TILLY** *with an evil smile.*)

EVIL GABBI. Okay! All you have to do to get into the awesome evil club is to makeout with me for one whole minute.

TILLY. What?

EVIL GABBI. What do you say?

TILLY. Uh –

> (*Hearing "uh,"* **EVIL TINA** *bears down on* **AGNES** *again.*)

AGNES. OWWW!

TILLY. Okay! Okay, I'll do it.

EVIL GABBI. Yummy.

> (**EVIL GABBI** *leans in.*)

> (**TILLY** *closes her eyes and leans forward to kiss* **EVIL GABBI**.)

> (*Suddenly, out of nowhere,* **EVIL TINA** *kicks* **TILLY** *in the face.*)

EVIL TINA. I knew you were gay!

EVIL GABBI. Hahaha! Dyke, you're so in love with me!

EVIL TINA. Here, why don't you make-out with your sister?

> (**EVIL TINA** *throws* **AGNES** *on top of* **TILLY**.)

EVIL GABBI. Oh God, you two are so gross.

> (**AGNES** *works her way back up to her feet.*)

AGNES. And you two are going to die!

> (*Both the Succubi smile and begin laughing.*)

> (*Their laughter becomes louder and louder. It consumes* **AGNES** *and* **TILLY** *who begin laughing as well. The laughing becomes more hysterical as*

both **TILLY** *and* **AGNES** *fall to the ground from painfully laughing so hard.)*

(It all suddenly stops.)

(The Succubi walk around looking at their victims.)

EVIL TINA. See you around. Lesbians.

(The Succubi girls skip away, ironically holding hands.)

*(**AGNES** gets up and walks over to **TILLY**.)*

AGNES. Hey. Are you okay?

TILLY. *(Really upset.)* No!

*(**TILLY** runs away. As she does, her awesome armor falls off and she slowly morphs from a teen to a little girl.)*

*(**AGNES** watches helplessly as her little sister dashes out of sight.)*

*(**CHUCK** appears back at his table.)*

AGNES. I thought you said Tillius was a guy.

CHUCK. *(Equally confused.)* He Is.

AGNES. Then why would her character get picked on like that?

*(**CHUCK** examines **TILLY** notebook and looks back at **AGNES**.)*

CHUCK. Look, I'm no Time Lord, but I don't think this module is just a game.

AGNES. What?

CHUCK. I think this is actually your sister's diary. She just wrote it in geek.

Scene Nine

(**AGNES** *wanders into The Gap looking for her BFF.*)

AGNES. Hey, Vera, we gotta talk.

You're not going to believe this, but –

(**AGNES** *is stopped when she sees "***LILITH***" standing there in the middle of The Gap looking at clothes.*)

(*However instead of being super badass gothy, this real-life* **LILITH** *is actually pretty mousey. She's modestly dressed in regular school clothes and glasses. Currently she's looking at herself in a full-length mirror.*)

(**AGNES** *looks around to make sure she's not in the D&D game. She slowly approaches* **LILITH**.)

(**LILITH** *sees* **AGNES** *in the mirror which startles her.*)

LILITH. Ah!

AGNES. Sorry!

LILITH. Can I help you?

AGNES. What are you doing here?

LILITH. What do you mean?

AGNES. What are you doing here?

LILITH. I work here.

AGNES. At the Gap?

LILITH. Why else would I being wearing so much denim?

AGNES. So you're real?

(**AGNES** *realizes she must sound crazy.*)

Sorry, you just sorta look like someone I sorta...don't know. That must sound crazy.

LILITH. No, not at all...that sounds completely – how can I help you exactly?

AGNES. I was just looking for my friend. She's usually the one working the changing rooms. Do you know where she is?

LILITH. Vera? She's…uh… I don't know. She sorta just took off and told me "Don't let anyone know I'm gone" thus why I'm now here instead folding things in the back.

AGNES. Sounds like her.

I should go. Let Vera know that I came by. My name's Agnes by the way

LILITH. Oh I know.

AGNES. You know?

LILITH. Sorry, that must sound weird. I don't mean to be weird. You wouldn't remember me, but we've met before.

I knew your sister Tilly. I mean – we were in the same class. I met you at the…uh –

AGNES. Right, your whole class came out. That was really sweet of you guys.

LILITH. She was awesome.

Like the best person I ever knew. Like ever.

I really mean it.

AGNES. Yeah?

LILITH. Yeah.

AGNES. I didn't catch your name.

LILITH. Oh. Sorry. I'm Lily.

(This tingles **AGNES***'s Spider-sense once again.)*

AGNES. Wait, your name's Lily?

LILITH. Yep.

AGNES. As in Lilith?

LILITH. Actually it's short for Elizabeth –

AGNES. So, wait, this was real.

LILITH. What was real?

AGNES. You and Tilly. You two were real.

LILITH. I'm not following –

AGNES. You two dated.

LILITH. WHAT!?!

No!

   *(**LILITH** is suddenly super upset.)*

AGNES. Oh my God, that totally explains it!

LILITH. I didn't date Tilly! I like boys. I swear. I would never...with a girl –

AGNES. Of course, you were together. It's so obvious. Look at you!

LILITH. No, we weren't!

AGNES. You don't have to hide it!

LILITH. I'm not.

AGNES. It's okay, you can tell me. TELL ME!

LILITH. I don't have anything to tell!

   *(**VERA**, hearing the commotion from across the store, runs up to her friend.)*

VERA. Hey! What's with all the excitement?

AGNES. This is Tilly's girlfriend!

LILITH. No, I'm not! I swear!

VERA. You should go. I'm so sorry. My friend has a brain thingy...it makes her sound crazy. You should leave before she starts with the mouth-foaming and the biting. GO!

   *(**VERA** pushes **LILITH** away.)*

What the hell's wrong with you?

AGNES. She was Tilly's girlfriend!

VERA. Okay, one, chill pill. Two, even if she was, we're in the middle of a Gap so you screaming out "you're a lesbo" in the middle of the changing area isn't the best way to coax her out of the closet. And, three, are those my gloves?

AGNES. I'm sorry. I just thought...that girl might be the only link I have left to –

(VERA grabs AGNES by her shoulders and looks her in the eyes to calm her down.)

VERA. I know, Agnes. But, look at me, whoever that chick is, she's still just a fifteen-year-old girl growing up in the middle of Ohio. If she's in the closet, she's gonna be in there deep.

Scene Ten

(**TILLY** *is seated next to a campfire. She's polishing her sword. She looks a bit sad.*)

(**AGNES** *cautiously approaches.*)

AGNES. Hey.

TILLY. Hey.

AGNES. What happened back there with the evil Cheer-o-stititutes?

TILLY. What did it look like?

AGNES. Did that sorta stuff really happen? I mean in real life?

TILLY. I was a dorky fifteen-year-old girl who loved D&D, what do you think?

AGNES. So how come you had to make up a game to tell me all this?

TILLY. I didn't want to tell you all this if that's what you're wondering. This game was supposed to be private.

AGNES. I met Lily, by the way. The real one.

(*This news stops* **TILLY** *doing what she's doing. She however does not make eye contact with* **AGNES.**)

TILLY. Oh yeah?

AGNES. She's gay, isn't she?

TILLY. Maybe. I don't know.

AGNES. Um. Are you?

TILLY. I...don't know.

AGNES. It must have been hard.

TILLY. I guess?

AGNES. Tilly, you can talk to me –

TILLY. (*Suddenly out of character.*) I'm not really her, you know?

(**CHUCK** *enters.*)

AGNES. What?

CHUCK. I'm not her.

AGNES. Chuck?

CHUCK. Look, I can only extrapolate so much, but this is feeling a bit blasphemous.

AGNES. I was talking to my sister, do you mind?

CHUCK. Agnes, I'm all for role-playing, but this is a bit deeper than I usually get.

AGNES. Play the role, Chuck.

CHUCK. But Agnes –

AGNES. PLAY IT!

CHUCK. *(Cautiously.)* Okay. Look, there's something in here that I think you should see –

AGNES. Do it in character.

CHUCK. Agnes –

AGNES. DO IT!

> *(**CHUCK** takes a deep breath.)*

CHUCK & TILLY. Agnes…

Can you do me a favor?

AGNES. What?

> *(**TILLY** pulls out the game module.)*

TILLY. I wrote something for Lily. In here.

> *(**TILLY** takes a sealed envelope that's been paper-clipped from inside the homespun module and hands it to **AGNES**.)*

> *("For Lily" is written across it.)*

Can you give it to her?

Scene Eleven

(**MILES** *rushes into the store and finds* **VERA** *who's at work folding shirts.*)

MILES. Hey, can I talk to you for a minute?

VERA. What are you doing here?

MILES. I need advice.

VERA. Yes. Those pants don't fit. You look ridiculous.

(**MILES** *is rocking some really baggy jeans.*)

MILES. That's not the advice I'm looking for.

VERA. No? Maybe it should be.

MILES. Look, you're my friend, right?

VERA. Nope. I'm your girlfriend's friend. I just stomach you because you're with my girl – that is – until she wises up and dumps your dumb ass.

(*Nerdy nerd* **STEVE** *approaches. He's holding a bundle of clothes in his hands.*)

STEVE. Hi. When you're done with him, could I get some help?

MILES. So she IS going to dump me?

VERA. (*To* **STEVE.**) How can I help you?

MILES. Agnes is cheating on me with a freshman!

VERA. (*To* **MILES.**) I wasn't talking to you! I was talking to –

STEVE. Steve.

VERA. Stephen here.

Stephen, how can I help you?

STEVE. Well, I was wondering if –

(**VERA** *looks at his piles of clothes.*)

VERA. Hold up. You're seriously not gonna buy these, right?

(*She examines his stack of clothes and throws piece by piece on the ground.*)

No. No. No.

Come with me.

(**VERA** *looks at the discarded clothes rack and starts filing through it.*)

MILES. What about me?

VERA. There is no you.

MILES. So you're fine with your best friend fooling around with a fish?

STEVE. What's a fish?

VERA. Derogatory term for a freshman. You're a freshman, right?

STEVE. Yep.

VERA. (*Cheery.*) I knew you looked familiar!

(*Suddenly serious.*)

Now take off your clothes.

STEVE. What?

(**VERA** *hands him a new shirt and pants she's pulled from the discard rack.*)

VERA. Put these on.

STEVE. Uh. Okay.

(**STEVE** *starts to change clothes right there in the middle of the store.*)

(**VERA** *stops him.*)

VERA. In the dressing room, dummy.

(**STEVE** *realizes his mistake and rushes offstage with the clothes.*)

MILES. So?

VERA. You're still here?

MILES. What do I do?

VERA. Break up with her.

MILES. Really?

VERA. Yes, really.

MILES. But I don't want to.

VERA. Oh come on. Be honest with me, Miles, you don't care about her. You only care that she's a cheerleader and you're a football jock and it fits nicely within your two-dimensional high school dating paradigm.

You're only into her because she makes good eye-candy.

MILES. That's not true.

VERA. Then how come you haven't dropped the L-bomb yet?

MILES. The... Lesbian bomb?

VERA. The Love-bomb, you idiot! You've been together over a year and all you've said to her so far is "I really really like you."

That girl deserves more than that – more than some dumb jock in oversized jeans.

MILES. I'm also class president.

VERA. Whatever. You're still just some dude. And she's Agnes. My Agnes. Your résumé has gotta to be far more impressive than that to impress me.

MILES. You don't think I appreciate her?

VERA. Not really.

MILES. So you think I'm standing here in the middle of The Gap fighting with her best friend because I just think she's cute? Are you crazy? Of course I "L-bomb" her. But Jesus, Vera, she lost her sister. There's other things on her mind than me.

I've just been taking it slow.

For her.

VERA. ...

MILES. You're not the only person in the world that wants to protect her.

(They silently stand there next to each other.)

Doesn't matter either way, because she's now dating a freshman.

VERA. Miles, she's not dating a freshmen.

MILES. I met him. She admitted it. He's her "secret friend."

VERA. Yeah, I know.

MILES. You know?

VERA. He's her Dungeon Master.

MILES. He brings her into a dungeon?

VERA. Jesus Christ, Miles, NO! He's a D&D dork. He's the guy who rolls the dice or whatever.

MILES. Wait, she's just playing D&D? Why?

VERA. Well, maybe you should ask her.

(STEVE steps out of the dressing room. He looks good. Damn good.)

STEVE. What do you think?

(MILES looks at STEVE. He's impressed.)

MILES. Holy crap, Vera. You're a magician.

(STEVE admires himself in the mirror.)

STEVE. It is I, the great playa Steve!

Scene Twelve

KALIOPE. What's wrong, Agnes the Ass-hatted? By the droop of your shoulders and your downward gaze, it would indicate you are troubled somehow.

AGNES. Wow. Observant.

KALIOPE. Was that sarcasm?

AGNES. No.

KALIOPE. My apologies, Agnes. Though we elves may have heightened speed, agility, strength, and attractiveness –

AGNES. Don't forget modesty.

KALIOPE. We're unfortunately lacking in "emotional awareness."

AGNES. So you're like a robot?

KALIOPE. No, we're elves. We're above emotions. That's a human trait.

AGNES. Well, color me envious right about now.

KALIOPE. What troubles you, Agnes the Ass-hatted?

AGNES. I joined this adventure to get to know my sister, to help her, but I don't think she needs me at all.

KALIOPE. Well, I don't think she needs help from most people. She IS a 20th level Paladin after all.
If anything, we travel with her for we often require her help.

AGNES. Wow, Elf, you're really bad at giving advice.

KALIOPE. I apologize. Would you like to copulate with me now?

AGNES. What?

KALIOPE. Copulate, fornicate, consensual intimate stimulus. I think it would make you feel better. I hear you humans like to do such things.

AGNES. CHUCK, I'm not going to fool around with the Elf-girl!

(**CHUCK** *suddenly appears.*)

CHUCK. What? I don't want to see you get sexy with the sexy Elf-girl. Why would I want to hear you describe that? Ew, gross, hot-girl on hot-girl action. I mean, that's so gay and I'm so...straight.

AGNES. Are you done?

> (AGNES *turns back to* KALIOPE *who leans in for a kiss.*)

Whoa, what are you doing?

KALIOPE & CHUCK. *(Whispers.)* Nothing!

AGNES. CHUCK!

CHUCK. Fine. Whatever.

You return back to your party who are all at the foot of the Mountain of Steepness. But before you can move forward, you spy something ahead of you.

It's big, cube-shaped, and gelatinous!

> (*Lights come up on a Gelatinous Cube as the rest of* AGNES*'s parts step up beside her.*)

AGNES. Ew, what is that?

KALIOPE. Oh that? That, my dear human friend, is Boss Number Two. Miles the Gelatinous Cube!

AGNES. What?

> (*Adventure* STEVE *leaps into the fray.*)

STEVE. It is I, the great Mage Steve and I've come to – oh neat, a jello-mold!

> (STEVE *goes to touch The Gelatinous Cube, but it sucks him down whole...*)

Ahhhhh!

> (*...And spits out bones and armor.*)

> (*The Cube burps.*)

AGNES. *(To* TILLY.*)* You made my boyfriend a jello-mold?

TILLY. What? No.

KALIOPE. You actually did.

LILITH. The Elf is correct, love. You indeed made Agnes the Ass-Hatted's love companion into a big cube of demonic gelatin.

ORCUS. So, hold up, that thing isn't edible?

KALIOPE. No.

ORCUS. Dammit, and I got the munchies!

AGNES. Why'd you make Miles a flesh-eating jello-mold?

TILLY. I don't know.

AGNES. Tilly!

TILLY. Maybe because he sucks.

AGNES. I thought you liked him.

TILLY. Yeah, I loved watching you two make out every day in our living room to that Cranberries CD.

AGNES. We weren't listening to the Cranberries. It was 10,000 Maniacs.

TILLY. Oh, I'm sorry, that's so much less lame.

AGNES. Whatever, he's my boyfriend!

TILLY. He's a fart-knocker.

AGNES. He liked you.

TILLY. He touched me.

(*Shocked silence.*)

AGNES. What?

(*Still shocked. Still silent.*)

TILLY. Okay, no, he didn't. But he mighta.

AGNES. That's not funny!

TILLY. "That's not funny."

AGNES. Seriously, that's not something to joke about.

TILLY. "Seriously, that's not something to joke about."

AGNES. Real mature.

TILLY. "Real mature."

AGNES. Stop that!

TILLY. "Stop that!"

(**LILITH** *steps in between the two squabbling sisters.*)

LILITH. Though I find you mocking your sister incredibly sexy, shouldn't we, you know, kill this thing before it kills us.

TILLY. You're right. Okay, team, let's kill Miles!

AGNES. Wait. No.

TILLY. See, and once again, you're choosing your boyfriend over me.

KALIOPE. Your boyfriend is a gelatinous cube?

ORCUS. Gross.

AGNES. This isn't fair, Tilly, and you know it.

TILLY. I thought you were here to save my soul. I guess you didn't mean it. Quest is over, guys! We lost. The last adventure I will ever take ended in a forfeit!

AGNES. Stop.

TILLY. Why? So I can watch you run off with Slimy McSlimerface over there and forget all about me?

AGNES. I would never forget about you.

TILLY. You did when I was alive.

(*This comeback cuts* **AGNES** *deep.*)

ORCUS. Oh snap, she went there.

TILLY. So are we giving up or what?

(**AGNES** *regains her composure.*)

AGNES. Fine. Whatever. It's clearly not my boyfriend, right? You just named him that. Miles isn't actually green, slimy, and cube-shaped.

LILITH. So are we going to kill it or not?

AGNES. Okay, let's fight it.

TILLY. Really?

AGNES. Really.

TILLY. Alright! You hear that, Miles! We're gonna kill the crap out of you and your dumb face!

AGNES. Can we not call it Miles?

TILLY. Sure. We don't have to call it Miles.

*(Suddenly the Gelatinous Cube magically transforms into the actual human **MILES**. Except this **MILES** is dressed like Conan the Barbarian and armed with a large broadsword.)*

AGNES. What the hell?

TILLY. Oh, I don't think Boss number two was actually a gelatinous cube.

LILITH. It's a shape-shifter.

KALIOPE. A doppelganger to be exact.

TILLY. So go kill it, sis. Yay!

*(**TILLY** pushes **AGNES** forward.)*

CHUCK. (VOICEOVER.) BOSS FIGHT NUMBER TWO: AGNES THE ASS-HATTED VERSUS MILES THE DOPPELGANGER!!!

AGNES. You're not actually him – you're not actually him.

MILES. Hey, baby, how ya doing? Did you see me score that touchdown?

*(**MILES** takes a swing at her. She dodges.)*

I was awesome!

AGNES. This is not fair, Tilly!

TILLY. It's a boss, it's not supposed to be fair.

AGNES. You're not actually Miles.

MILES. Don't tell me who I am!

*(**MILES** takes another large swing at her. **AGNES** dodges it last minute, but falls to the ground. She's now on her bum.)*

AGNES. Seriously, are you guys not going to help?

LILITH, KALIOPE, ORCUS, TILLY. *(Ad-libbing.)* No, not really. You look like you got it handled. I don't want to step in between a lovers' quarrel. It's really none of my business.

AGNES. You guys suck.

MILES. Hey, baby, since you're down there, why don't you "say hello to my little friend."

(He gives her a smirk.)

(He then suddenly takes a final swing at her, this time she blocks his blade with her own.)

AGNES. Actually, asshole, I don't care who you look like, nobody disrespects me!

*(**AGNES** kicks him in the stomach. He falls back.)*

Let's go.

*(Back on her feet, **AGNES** attacks **MILES**. Their blades clash back and forth in an impressive array of swordplay. With her smaller weapon, **AGNES** is able to attack quickly, putting **MILES** in a defensive posture.)*

*(However when he gets a swing in, his heavier sword knocks **AGNES**'s blade clear out of her hands.)*

(He takes a few swipes at her while she's defenseless, she luckily avoids most of them, except for one that slashes her in the arm.)

AGNES Ahh!

*(He tries to stab her through, but overcommits his attack. **AGNES** disarms him.)*

*(**AGNES** now rears back and punches him in the stomach, in the chest, and in the face. None of the hits bother him.)*

MILES. You can't hurt me! I play football.

AGNES. Oh yeah. Well, welcome to my foot, balls!

*(**AGNES** kicks **MILES** in the junk.)*

(He keels over. She breaks his neck.)

(He dies.)

TILLY. Wow. And I was just starting to like that guy. Aw, too bad. Let's go!

Scene Thirteen

(As **AGNES** *begins walking, "*EVIL TINA*" and "*EVIL GABBI*" run up to her.)*

(Except here they aren't actually "evil" in this moment, they're just students. No wings or horns or bloody mouths, just regular cheerleaders. And they're super chipper and nice.)

EVIL TINA. Hello, Agnes!

EVIL GABBI. Hi!

EVIL TINA. Do you have a minute?

EVIL GABBI. Just one free minute?

EVIL TINA & EVIL GABBI. Please please please!!!

AGNES. Uh okay. Sure. What's up?

EVIL TINA. I'm Tina.

EVIL GABBI. And I'm Gabbi.

EVIL TINA. And we're both on this year's yearbook committee representing the Freshmen class and we wondering if it'd be okay if we ran an ad in this year's Bobcat Annual.

AGNES. Why would I care what you do?

EVIL GABBI. Well, it's not an ad for us, silly!

EVIL TINA. It's just by us.

EVIL GABBI. For Tilly.

EVIL TINA & EVIL GABBI. Your sister.

AGNES. I know who my sister is.

EVIL TINA. We wanted to do one for her last year at our Junior High, but it was already off to the printer by the time –

EVIL GABBI. Tragedy stuck.

EVIL TINA. So we couldn't.

EVIL GABBI. So we thought we'd do one this year.

EVIL TINA. To show that she'll always be part of the Class of '99.

EVIL GABBI. That she'll always be one of us.

EVIL TINA & EVIL GABBI. And that we love her.

AGNES. So you were friends with my sister?

EVIL GABBI. Of course.

EVIL TINA. She was such a good spirit.

EVIL GABBI. She always knew how to make someone smile.

EVIL TINA. We were both just devastated when it happened. I mean we didn't hang out as much as we should, but –

EVIL TINA & EVIL GABBI. We both consider her a very close friend.

(Both girls give AGNES *a big smile.)*

AGNES. Is that right?

(They nod cheerfully.)

EVIL TINA. We admired her.

EVIL GABBI. Like we admire you.

AGNES. You admire me?

EVIL GABBI. We are fellow cheerleaders, right? I mean we're freshmen and you're on the Varsity squad, but we're all fellow Bobcats, right?

AGNES. Right.

EVIL TINA. So we're like sisters.

EVIL GABBI. Totally sisters!

AGNES. Yeah. And me being on the voting panel for who makes it to JV from the Freshman squad would have nothing to do with this, correct?

EVIL TINA. No, not at all!

EVIL GABBI. As we said, we were gonna do this last year but we ran out of time.

AGNES. What about Tillius? What did you think of Tillius?

EVIL TINA. Um, who?

EVIL GABBI. Was she one of your sister's friends?

AGNES. Yeah, you guys were real super close.

EVIL TINA. So what do you think?

AGNES. Can I see your yearbook there?

(AGNES grabs it and violently throws it against the walls. The pages fly everywhere.)

AGNES. GET THE HELL OUT OF MY FACE! NOW!!! Before I rip your stupid eyeballs out.

EVIL TINA. Okay!

EVIL GABBI. Sorry to bother you!

(The two girls run away.)

(TILLY enters.)

TILLY. That seemed really effective.

AGNES. What am I supposed to do, Tilly? I can't just beat them up.

TILLY. I woulda.

(AGNES starts to walk away.)

Agnes…

Agnes…

Are you still mad at me for making you kill your boyfriend?

(AGNES stares at the ghost of her sister standing there.)

AGNES. Am I going crazy?

TILLY. It's better than being dead.

Scene Fourteen

(Later that day. **AGNES** *is back at the game shop, staring at the game map that* **CHUCK** *has drawn out. She's trying to figure out where they left off.)*

AGNES. So where were we?

CHUCK. Well, you're right here.
You and your party are climbing the Mountain of Steepness when suddenly you run back into –

*(***MILES*** enters the game shop.)*

MILES. Hey.

CHUCK. – your boyfriend? No, that's not right.

AGNES. Hey.

MILES. Am I interrupting anything?

CHUCK. Well, sorta.

MILES. Were you guys playing… Dungeons and Dragons?

AGNES. Yeah.

MILES. Cool.

AGNES. We weren't making out if that's what you were wondering.

CHUCK. What? That was an option?

AGNES. No.

MILES. Vera told you, huh?

AGNES. Yep.

MILES. I misinterpreted.

AGNES. With a freshman?

MILES. Well, he is a really big freshman.

CHUCK. I'm not big. Maybe you're just small.

MILES. What?

CHUCK. Nothing!

MILES. Are you mad at me?

AGNES. I'm not happy.

MILES. Okay, that's fair, but you're not mad.

AGNES. Well, keep asking me that question and we'll see.

MILES. Well, I came by because I thought, maybe we could, you know, hang out.

AGNES. I'm busy.

MILES. You're just playing a game.

AGNES. It's more than that.

MILES. Can it not wait for just one night?

AGNES. No.

(*AGNES shoots him a glare.*)

(*He cautiously re-approaches.*)

MILES. Well, okay, how about tomorrow? Can we hang out tomorrow?

AGNES. I don't know…

MILES. I thought you said you weren't mad.

AGNES. I'm not mad. I'm just focused on this right now.

MILES. Agnes, come on.

AGNES. I'm not in the mood to –

(*CHUCK tries to help –.*)

CHUCK. Hey man, do you want to play?

MILES. What?

AGNES. Huh?

CHUCK. Do you want to play? I mean if you want to hang out, let's hang. I mean you can't do any worse than Agnes here, right? She sucks.

AGNES. He doesn't want to play.

(*MILES looks at CHUCK, the game, and AGNES.*)

MILES. Actually, I would. I would like to play, Chuck.

AGNES. What are you doing?

MILES. This is important to you and I want to be part of it.

AGNES. It's private though.

MILES. I know. But you never talk to me about your sister. I just…if this could help me get to know you better, I wanna try. Please.

AGNES. You're for real?

MILES. I am.

> *(AGNES thinks it over.)*

AGNES. Fine. Roll him up a character sheet.

> *(MILES gives CHUCK a smile.)*

> *(CHUCK rolls the D&D dice which transforms the world back into...)*

LILITH. Agnes, look out!

KALIOPE. Boss Number Two!

> *(AGNES stands in between MILES and her party.)*

AGNES. It's okay!

ORCUS. Dude, if that thing is that hard to kill, I give up now.

AGNES. NO! This is not Boss Number Two. This is Miles. The real Miles. My boyfriend.

TILLY. *(Suddenly annoyed.)* What's he doing here?

AGNES. He wanted to come.

TILLY. We already have five people in our party.

AGNES. He just wanted to get to know you – us – better.

TILLY. It's not really the same thing, now is it?

> *(LILITH walks up to MILES and begins sniffing him.)*

LILITH. Can I eat him? He looks meaty.

> *(MILES steps away from the demon-girl.)*

MILES. So this is Dungeons and Dragons, huh? Neat.

TILLY. You're not serious.

AGNES. Look, you may not like him, but at least I know he has my back.

TILLY. We have your back.

AGNES. Right, just like you had my back when you made me KILL MY BOYFRIEND?

MILES. You killed me?

AGNES. No, I just killed a big fat blob that looked like you.

MILES. I look like a big fat blob?

TILLY. If you got in trouble, we would have stepped in.

KALIOPE. Assuredly.

LILITH. I wouldn't have.

ORCUS. No way.

TILLY. Guys, you're not helping.

(*AGNES rolls her eyes and walks away.*)

AGNES. So what's the next thing we have to fight?

KALIOPE. The next boss is a Beholder.

AGNES. Aw, that sounds cute. Like "Beauty is in the eye of…"

(*TILLY, KALIOPE, ORCUS, and LILITH look at each other.*)

TILLY, KALIOPE, ORCUS, LILITH. (*Ad-libbingly.*) No. Nope. Not the same thing at all. That thing is ugly. Like just one big scary eyeball with teeth ugly.

(*MILES runs up to AGNES to relieve her of her fears.*)

MILES. Trust me, babe. Whatever it is, we're going to be fine. I'm here now.

(*Explosion!!!*)

(*The Succubi are back.*)

(*TILLY, KALIOPE, ORCUS, LILITH, and AGNES all fall into defensive stances as MILES just stands there.*)

EVIL GABBI. Oh my God, Evil Tina, look! An impenetrable wall of gay.

EVIL TINA. How will we ever get passed them?

AGNES. Miles, get back!

MILES. Why?

TILLY. Get back behind us, dummy!

MILES. Guys, they're just cheerleaders. What are they going to do?

> (**EVIL TINA** *and* **EVIL GABBI** *let out a little cute schoolgirl laugh...*)

EVIL TINA & EVIL GABBI. Heeheehee!

> (*...And then rips out his heart.*)

> (**MILES** *falls to the ground dead.*)

EVIL TINA. Yummy, I was looking for a snack.

TILLY. Well, he didn't last long.

> (**AGNES** *grabs* **TILLY** *by the arm.*)

AGNES. Tilly, shoot them with a magic missile.

TILLY. I can't.

AGNES. What do you mean you can't?

TILLY. I forgot the spell.

AGNES. What do you mean you forgot the spell?

TILLY. It's a thing. A D&D thing. It's not going to help us.

> (*The Succubus twins begin circling their prey.*)

EVIL GABBI. How hungry are you, Evil Tina?

EVIL TINA. Starving.

EVIL GABBI. What would you like first? Light or dark meant?

EVIL TINA. I'm in the mood for...geek.

> (*They both start towards* **TILLY**.*)

LILITH. I suggest we stop these Succubi the old fashion way.

AGNES. And that would be?

LILITH. With violence, love. Lots and lots of violence.

> (*They all raise their weapons.*)

EVIL GABBI. Oh no, what will we fight them with?

EVIL TINA. We're so unarmed.

> (*Suddenly, Adventurer* **STEVE** *arrives on the scene with two long blades in each hand.*)

STEVE. It is I, the great Mage **STEVE**, returned to do battle with…

> *(The Succubi rip off **STEVE**'s arms and take his weapons. He obviously dies. Again.)*

EVIL TINA. I guess that answers that.

> *(**TILLY**'s party attacks.)*

> *(However, the Succubi – though demonically cutesy – are total badasses.)*

> *(The fastest in the party, **KALIOPE** and **LILITH**, rush at the devil girls. Their weapons clash into the Succubis' swords in an array of cuts and parries. However, before the elf and demon-princess can score a hit, both the succubi unfurl their wings and use them to strike down their opponents.)*

> *(**ORCUS** begins lifting heavy rocks and heaves them at their enemy which forces the evil cheerleaders to take to the air.)*

> *(Most of **ORCUS**'s stones fly off-target, but even those on-target have zero effect as the evil cheerleaders just kick them in mid-air right back at him. One of which strikes him in the head knocking him to the ground.)*

> *(The evil cheerleaders laugh and high-five.)*

> *(Suddenly, sisters **AGNES** and **TILLY** attack. They both let out screams which gets the demon-girls' attention just in time for them to send well-timed kicks to the sisters' faces.)*

> *(They both hit the ground with a thud.)*

> *(The evil cheerleaders begin towards the fallen **TILLY**.)*

EVIL TINA Awww, look at the little nerd girl.

EVIL GABBI. Are you going to pee your pants, nerd girl.

EVIL TINA. Don't worry, dyke, your pain is about to end!

(EVIL TINA rears back her sword to strike down TILLY.)

(Seeing her love in trouble, LILITH rushes over to protect her!)

LILITH. No!

(However as she rushes them, the Succubi easily avoid her desperate attack and stab her through.)

(Looking at the open wound on her torso, LILITH falls to the ground motionless.)

TILLY. LILITH!!!

EVIL TINA. Awww, did your girlfriend just die?

EVIL GABBI. Aw, that's so sad. Aren't they just so sad?

(They both laugh mockingly at TILLY and the slain LILITH.)

(As the Succubus twins laugh, AGNES, KALIOPE, and ORCUS get back on their feet behind them.)

AGNES. I don't see what's so funny.

ORCUS. You'll just be joining her in two seconds.

KALIOPE. Prepare to be ushered to your deaths.

(EVIL TINA and EVIL GABBI roll their evil eyes.)

EVIL TINA. You can't beat us.

EVIL GABBI. We're way too powerful for you.

(AGNES steps forward.)

AGNES. Who said we were going to do it with our fists?

(The smirks on the Succubis' faces suddenly disappear.)

EVIL TINA. What do you mean?

(AGNES tosses away her sword and shield.)

AGNES. Enough with all this dorky swordfighting stuff –

(She begins applying on some lipstick.)

You really think you're badasses? Then let's finish this…

(She sticks out her hands as **KALIOPE** *and* **ORCUS** *puts pom-poms into them.)*

AGNES. Cheerleader style.

We challenge you to…a dance battle.

(Lightning and thunder!!!!)

CHUCK. BONUS ROUND: AGNES, THE ELF, AND ORCUS VERSUS THE EVIL SUCCUBI CHEERLEADERS IN A DANCE BATTLE!!!

(The Succubi smile in agreement.)

(Music like C&C Music Factory's "Gonna Make You Sweat"* fills the world around them as the two crews go at it in a full-on cheerleader-esque dance battle.)

*(***AGNES***'s crew starts it out. They look okay… somewhat comedic and funny, but nothing too terribly terrible.)*

(The two Succubi, unimpressed, step up and start doing an elaborate cheerleading/hip-hop fusion routine that completely kills it. It's truly truly truly outrageous.)

(Thinking they've won, the Succubi raise their arms in victory. When they do, **AGNES** *and company pick up their weapons and drive it through their unsuspecting enemies.)*

EVIL TINA. No fair!

EVIL GABBI. You cheated.

*(***AGNES*** smiles coyly.)*

---

*A license to produce *She Kills Monsters Young Adventurers Edition* does not include a performance license for "Gonna Make You Sweat." The publisher and author suggest that the licensee contact ASCAP or BMI to ascertain the rights holder to acquire permission for performance of this song. If permission is unattainable, the licensee should create an original composition in a similar style. For further information, please see music use note on page 3

AGNES. What? You really thought we were gonna dance battle you to death. Wow, I guess my sister's right. Cheerleaders *are* dumb.

> *(AGNES kills them both.)*

> *(AGNES turns back to TILLY and LILITH.)*

> *(Seeing TILLY cry over LILITH is too much for her.)*

AGNES Can we resurrect her?

KALIOPE. No. Tillius used that spell to save you.

AGNES. But you're magical, do something.

KALIOPE. I don't have that kind of magic.

AGNES. Orcus?

ORCUS. I only keep souls. I don't put them back.

AGNES. CHUCK!

> *(As if magically summoned, CHUCK and the gaming table suddenly appear.)*

CHUCK. What?

AGNES. Bring her back.

CHUCK. I can't.

AGNES. You killed her girlfriend, now bring her back.

CHUCK. I didn't kill her. She jumped in the way. I rolled the dice, it says she died.

AGNES. Screw the dice, just bring her back!

CHUCK. I can't. Not for this adventure. There's rules.

AGNES. What rules? You're the DM, you make the rules.

CHUCK. No, I don't. Gary Gygax made the rules.

AGNES. Who the hell is Gary Gygax?

CHUCK. He's the one who made the game.

AGNES. I don't care what you have to do, Chuck. Just bring her back. Now.

> *(The deceased MILES sits up from where he's been lying dead the whole time.)*

MILES. Hey, babe. Um, maybe you should take a breather. I just died and I'm fine.

AGNES. No, I'm not going to let my sister just suffer like this.

MILES. It's not actually your sister.

AGNES. Screw you!

MILES. Babe.

AGNES. Are you going to bring her back?

CHUCK. I'm sorry.

AGNES. No! Wrong answer!

(**AGNES** *violently pushes all the D&D game pieces off the table.*)

MILES. Agnes…

(*The ghost of* **TILLY** *enters.*)

TILLY. Stop.

AGNES. Go away.

TILLY. They're right, you know.

AGNES. Shut up.

TILLY. It's just a game.

AGNES. I was getting to know you. I was just starting to get to know you.

(**MILES,** *who can't hear* **TILLY**'s *part of the conversation, cautiously approaches.*)

MILES. Getting to know who, babe?

TILLY. My character's not dead.

AGNES. But you are.

TILLY & MILES. Agnes.

AGNES. This is a stupid game and you're not real and none of this matters because you died.

TILLY & CHUCK. Agnes.

AGNES. Chuck, I'm done.

CHUCK. What?

AGNES. Thank you so much for indulging me.
Really.
It was…something.

I'll call you if I change my mind.
But I'm done talking to ghosts.
Goodbye.

Scene Fifteen

(The next day.)

*(**VERA** approaches **AGNES** who's sitting quietly in study hall. **VERA** sits down next to her.)*

VERA. Miles says you had a bit of a meltdown.

AGNES. Miles needs to mind his own business.

VERA. What's up?

AGNES. Nothing.

VERA. Girl, it's me. I'm not your stupid boyfriend. Talk to me.

AGNES. It's stupid.

VERA. Agnes…

AGNES. It was just…that game was all I had of her.

Just a stupid character sheet and whatever she left scribbled out in that notebook.

VERA. That's not true – you have your memories –

AGNES. My memories? Right.

Do you want to know what my memories of Tilly are?

They're of this little nerdy girl who I never talked to, who I ignored, who I didn't understand because she didn't live in the same world as I did. Her world was filled with evil jello-molds and demon queens while mine…has Dave Matthews and cute haircuts. I didn't get her. I assumed one day I would – that she'd grow out of all this – that I'd be able to sit around and ask her about normal things like clothes and TV shows and boys…and as it turns out, no one even knows if she was even into boys or not.

VERA. It's okay, Agnes.

AGNES. No, it's not.

I didn't know her, Vera. I remember her as a baby, I remember her as this little toddler I loved picking up and holding, but I don't remember her as a teen at all. I'll never get the chance to know her as an adult.

And now all I have left is this stupid piece of paper and this stupid made-up adventure about killing a stupid made-up dragon.

VERA. Agnes, baby…

AGNES. It just all infinitely sucks.

> (**CHUCK** *enters the library and approaches.*)

CHUCK. Agnes – um, do you have a moment?

AGNES. What do you want?

CHUCK. I wanted to return this to you.

> (**CHUCK** *lays* **TILLY**'s *module carefully onto the library table.*)

AGNES. Thank you.

CHUCK. I was also wondering if you were free this afternoon.

AGNES. Are you asking me out?

CHUCK. I can do that?

VERA. She was being sarcastic, dummy.

AGNES. What is it, Chuck?

CHUCK. I just wanted to show you something. It's something of Tilly's.

AGNES. What?

> (*A spotlight falls onto a door as* **VERA** *exits the scene.*)

Where is this?

CHUCK. This is a friend's house.

AGNES. Who?

> (**CHUCK** *knocks on the door.*)

> (*As the door opens, the world shifts from darkness to* **RONNIE**'s *house.*)

> (*On the other side is* **ORCUS**…*but dressed as a normal sloppy High School kid named* **RONNIE**.*)

ORCUS. What's up, home-slice!

AGNES. Orcus?

CHUCK. Actually…this is Ronnie.

ORCUS. Hey, wow.

    Senior girl.

    At my house.

    Sweet.

CHUCK. *(To **AGNES**.)* I just wanted you to meet some of Tilly's friends.

        *(To **RONNIE**.)*

    Ronnie, this is who I was telling you about.

ORCUS. Whoa, you're Tilly's sister?

CHUCK. Yeah.

ORCUS. Man, you are a total Betty!

CHUCK. Dude.

ORCUS. What?

CHUCK. Outside voice.

ORCUS. I'm saying stuff outloud I should just keep in my head again, right?

    My bad.

    But look at that body.

CHUCK. So is your sister around?

ORCUS. Yeah. Lemme get her.

    You guys can come in if you want, just don't touch the TV, I'm recording Power Rangers!

AGNES. You really didn't do much to make him different.

        (CHUCK *takes a picture off a mantle and hands it to **AGNES**.)*

CHUCK. That's a picture of his sister.

        (AGNES *looks at it and realizes who it is…)*

AGNES. Kaliope.

CHUCK. Kelly, actually.

AGNES. Wow, is she actually hotter in real life?

CHUCK. Yep.

AGNES. How come I never noticed her at school?

CHUCK. Well…

> (RONNIE [ORCUS] *returns with his sister. She walks in using fore-arm crutches to help stabilize her cerebral palsy.*)

KALIOPE. What's up, Chuck?

CHUCK. Hey there, hot stuff.

KALIOPE. Who's this?

CHUCK. Tilly's sister.

KALIOPE. Oh, hi! Nice to meet you.

AGNES. Uh…hi.

> (*Shocked,* AGNES *blatantly stares at* KALIOPE*'s legs.*)

KALIOPE. What? Do I have something on my shoes?

AGNES. (*Suddenly embarrassed.*) Oh God, I'm so sorry, I didn't mean to –

KALIOPE. It's okay. I'm used to it.

> (KALIOPE *smiles at* AGNES.)

> (AGNES *returns it.*)

AGNES. So you play D&D with these guys?

KALIOPE. Yeah, well. My brother's always been into it, but it was actually Tilly that convinced me give it a shot. I know it's dorky, right?

AGNES. Yeah, I guess.

KALIOPE. Your sister was awesome. We loved her. We really miss her.

AGNES. Me too.

> (TILLY *enters.*)

TILLY. What are you doing?

> (AGNES *turns to* TILLY. *As she does, the world behind her disappears.*)

> (*The two girls are now in the middle of a dark void, only lit by two small pools of light.*)

AGNES. I'm getting to know your friends.

TILLY. Are you judging them?

AGNES. No.

TILLY. I know they're geeky, I'm geeky, we're all geeks.

AGNES. Why do you think I care about that stuff?

TILLY. Everyone else does or did. I mean until I got hit by a car and then suddenly, wow, I'm the most popular girl in school.

AGNES. Is that why all you guys play this?

TILLY. No, we play it because it's awesome. It's about adventures and saving the world and having magic. And maybe – I guess – in some small teeny capacity, it might have a little to do with wish fulfillment. Kelly gets to walk without crutches, Ronnie gets to be super strong...

AGNES. What about you?

TILLY. Me?

I get to save the princess.

(The real-life geeky **LILITH** *suddenly appears in her own pool of light. She's eating lunch alone.)*

*(***AGNES*** *sees her and approaches.)*

AGNES. Hi.

LILITH. Hi.

AGNES. Can we talk for a minute? I promise I'm not going to do anything crazy.

LILITH. Okay.

AGNES. Look, I'm sorry about freaking out the other day at your job, but –

LILITH. It's okay.

AGNES. Look, I know you're not gay or were my sister's whatever, but she wanted you to have this. It's a letter she wrote to you.

LILITH. What does it say?

AGNES. I don't know. It wasn't written to me.

Do you want it?

LILITH. Yes.

>   (**LILITH** *immediately grabs it, opens it, and reads it to herself.*)
>
>   (*When she's done, she looks up to* **AGNES.** *Her eyes are now full of tears.*)

Thank you.

AGNES. Have a good day.

>   (**AGNES** *turns to go.*)

LILITH. Wait.

>   (**AGNES** *stops.*)

I, uh… I did know Tilly.

AGNES. I know. You were at her funeral.

LILITH. No, I mean…we were close.
I mean, she wasn't my girlfriend or anything.
But she was my friend. Maybe my only real friend.
Cause she knew.
And she didn't judge me for it.
Even when everyone made fun of her for being my buddy. And called her names. And bullied her. She didn't care.

AGNES. So was she also…

LILITH. Does it matter?

AGNES. No. I guess not.

LILITH. She was my hero, Agnes. She saved me.
I loved her.
I just wish I could have told her that.

AGNES. Yeah, I know what you mean.

>   (**LILITH** *smiles, gets up, and walks away with tears now freely falling down her face.*)

(*To herself.*) Okay, Chuck, I get it.
Let's do this.

>   (*Suddenly the world changes to –.*)

Scene Sixteen

(ORCUS, KALIOPE, and TILLY are all standing beside AGNES.)

(CHUCK is back in his DM seat.)

CHUCK. (VOICEOVER.) BOSS NUMBER THREE!!!!

(All the fighters draw their weapons.)

(VOICEOVER.) VERA THE BEHOLDER!!!

(VERA THE BEHOLDER, a ferocious single eye-balled monster with sharp sharklike teeth, floats into the space.)

VERA. PUNY ADVENTURERS! YOU HAVE NO HOPE TO DEFEAT ME! I AM A BEHOLDER!!! AND I WILL –

(AGNES stabs it directly in its pupil.)

(It dies.)

AGNES. Well, that was super easy.

(AGNES turns back to her team.)

So where's this dragon Tiamat?

This is the right Castle of Evil, right?

TILLY. Yes, it's the right castle.

AGNES. So where is it?

TILLY. Well, Agnes, there's something you should know about Tiamat.

AGNES. And that is?

TILLY. It's a shapeshifter.

ORCUS. Like Miles the Gelatinous Cube.

AGNES. Okay?

KALIOPE. So it can take any form.

TILLY. A friend.

ORCUS. A lover.

KALIOPE. Anyone.

(Suddenly STEVE the Adventurer bounds in.)

STEVE. It is I, the great mage Steve!

> (**AGNES** *quickly pulls out a knife and throws it at him.*)

> (*It slams into* **STEVE**'s *head and kills him instantly.*)

AGNES. Take that, you…dragon?

> (**STEVE** *does not move.*)

He's, um, not getting back up.

KALIOPE. He's not Tiamat.

AGNES. If he's not then who is?

> (*From a long staircase, the shadow of a dark warrior slowly enters the room.*)

> (*It's their supposed dead friend* **LILITH**.)

LILITH. I don't know, love. Where could you possibly find a monster in this game?

AGNES. Lilith?

LILITH. I mean, look around, where oh where can all the monsters be?

> (*Looking around,* **AGNES** *starts to realize that all the "heroes" she's been with have been traditional D&D monsters all along.*)

> (**TILLY** *pulls* **AGNES** *back and points at* **ORCUS***!*)

TILLY. Watch out, Agnes! It's a demon!

> (**ORCUS** *however accusingly points at* **KALIOPE***!*)

ORCUS. A dark elf!

> (*In kind,* **KALIOPE** *points at* **LILITH***!*)

KALIOPE. A Demon Queen!

> (**AGNES** *raises up her sword between herself and her former companions. However they all turn to* **AGNES** *and* **TILLY** *and slowly raise their fingers at* **AGNES**'s *little sister.*)

LILITH, ORCUS, KALIOPE. Tiamat.

(Hearing this, AGNES turns to catch eyes with TILLY.)

(TILLY is giving her a devilish grin.)

TILLY. What? You didn't actually think I was a paladin, did you? Everyone knows paladins can't shoot magic missiles.

(Clearly, AGNES did not know this...)

AGNES. Sure. Yeah. Everybody knows... WHAT?

(TILLY lets out a laugh. However it's deep and demonic. This scares AGNES.)

Um, Tilly, what's happening?

TILLY. What do you think is happening, "Big Sis"? This is a D&D adventure. And what would a D&D adventure be if you didn't get to fight a dragon?

(TILLY hands her sword to AGNES.)

AGNES. Um... Chuck?

CHUCK. *(VOICEOVER.)* FINAL FIGHT!
AGNES.
VERSUS.
TIAMAT!!!

(STEVE now rises to feet and joins the other four evil adventurers.)

(They all give evil grins as they walk backwards into the shadows.)

(AGNES is alone.)

(Suddenly, the world goes black.)

(Then there's footsteps. Large, heavy footsteps.)

(In the darkness, the screech of something large and reptilian screams out.)

(And then there's eyes. Giant bright red glowing eyes. Five sets of them.)

(From the dark fog and haze, Tiamat emerges from the shadows. The stage is filled with smoke.)

AGNES. Oh God.

(Suddenly Tiamat attacks! **AGNES** *leaps out of the way and strikes out at the giant beast.)*

(She slashes it in the neck, face, and body, which only sends sparks flying. Her strikes do nothing against it.)

(Tiamat flails its wings at her. One of them strikes her, sending **AGNES** *flying across the room like a rag-doll. She slams into a wall and then onto the ground. She's clearly out of her league.)*

(Tiamat snaps at her. She uses her shield from being bitten, but as she gets occupied fighting one head, another slings in and strikes her in the ribs.)

(They bite at her, grabbing onto her limbs. They breath fire [or compressed air] at her.)

(She shields herself for the fire and kicks away at the snapping heads.)

(The large beast and **AGNES** *wage an all out war against one another. It's an impressive and spectacular fight.)*

(And in the greatest fight ever to be seen on a theatrical stage, **AGNES** *summons the strength to survive. She plunges her sword deep into the heart of the beast.)*

(It rears back all of its heads into the air in anguish as it thrashes around in a loud, and explosive death.)

(The dragon finally collapses onto the stage dead.)

(However…it's not over.)

(From the smoke and shadows, a new figure slowly emerges.)

(Seeing it, **AGNES** *picks up her blade to defend herself until she sees who it is.)*

(It's **TILLY.** *The real* **TILLY.** *Now dressed like her little sister instead of the warrior princess.)*

(Seeing this, **AGNES**'s *eyes begin to fill with tears as her little sister approaches.)*

TILLY. Good job.

AGNES. Tilly?

TILLY. So did you have fun?

AGNES. What?

TILLY. Did you have fun? That's the point in all this. Did you have fun?

> **(AGNES,** *not knowing how to respond, simply nods her head.)*

Good.

> **(TILLY** *begins to exits.)*

AGNES. Wait.

> **(TILLY** *stops.)*

You're not real. You're gone.

TILLY. Yes. But this story remains. And isn't that essentially all that life is – a collection of stories? This is one of mine…

> *(The rest of* **TILLY**'s *party re-emerge from the shadows.)*

KALIOPE. …and not just some story that I experienced like a party or a dance or an event, but something I dreamt –

LILITH. Something far more personal and important than happenstance. This story came from my soul and by breathing life into it, who knows?

ORCUS. Maybe a bit of my soul gets the chance to breathe for a moment once again.

CHUCK. *(Reading from the module.)* I love you, my sister.

TILLY. I'm sorry I can't be there.

CHUCK. *(Reading from the module.)* I have no idea why you had to experience this adventure alone without me. But I hope it gave you a glimpse into me the way I wanted you to see me –

ORCUS. Strong…

LILITH. Powerful…

KALIOPE. And magical.

CHUCK. *(Closing the module.)* Congratulations, you have finished the Quest for the Lost Soul of Athens.

> (**TILLY** *and* **AGNES** *finally hug.*)

NARRATOR *(Voiceover.)* And so… Agnes the Ass-hatted accomplished her very first quest. Soon she would embark on another and then another and so forth and so on for the rest of her life. Miles the boyfriend who would one day become Miles the ex-boyfriend and then just Miles the friend would join her on her many quests alongside Chuck the Big Brain'd and Tilly's old group of friends, Ronnie the Slacker, Kelly the not-so-good-legged, and Lily the Closeted. Tilly was never forgotten, Agnes went to college, and soon the world finally embraced geeks not as outsiders, but as awesome.

Agnes eventually moved out of that average small town and brought the many memories of an average life with her. And this made her happy.

> *(Lights down.)*

End of Play